ZANDER

A PERFECTLY INDEPENDENT SERIES NOVELLA

AMANDA SHELLEY

Visit my website at
www.amandashelley.com

CONNECT WITH AMANDA SHELLEY

Want to be the first to know about upcoming sales and new releases? Make sure you sign up for my newsletter as well as connect with me on social media and your favorite retail store.

Website:
www.amandashelley.com
Newsletter:
https://geni.us/AmandaShelleyNL
Facebook:
https://www.facebook.com/authoramandashelley/
Instagram:
https://www.instagram.com/authoramandashelley/
Reader's Group:
https://www.facebook.com/groups/AmandasArmyofReaders/
Tik Tok:
https://www.tiktok.com/@authoramandashelley
Amazon:
https://www.amazon.com/author/amandashelley
Goodreads:
https://www.goodreads.com/author/show/19713563.Aman
da_Shelley

Book Bub:

https://www.bookbub.com/profile/amanda-shelley

ABOUT THE BOOK

Zander

A Perfectly Independent Series Novella

About the Book

Zander's known for being a player both on and off the court. When his name shows up as my next client, my heart stalls, and not in a good way. There's no way I'll survive the semester with him. I just don't have the patience.

However, when I need help, Zander makes a proposal I can't refuse. He'll be my fake date to my best friend's wedding so I don't have to face my ex and his new girlfriend alone.

The weekend goes off without a hitch as we effortlessly pretend to have the time of our lives.

All is perfect... until I realize my feelings for Zander are no longer an act.

What will I do when our arrangement comes to an end?

1

ZANDER

AS I RUSH from the gym to my first class, I'll admit I'm anxious. Not only am I on the verge of being late, but today we're getting our first paper back. I must pass this class and the next to graduate, but with the season well underway to get us back into the championships the pressure is on.

Usually, when pressure builds, I handle it. I'm an excellent multi-tasker and always keep my eye on the prize. But in this particular class, when the pressure hits—so does my dyslexia. Give me numbers, I'm your man. I easily pass advanced math courses in my sleep. Make me read articles on psychological studies and write ten-page essays, yeah not so much. Don't get me wrong, I can do them, but I need extended time—which is something I'm short on with extra practices, watching tape of my competitors, and keeping up with my other courses.

Since freshman year, I've had a tutor who reads all course material that isn't already digital aloud for me. I can read, but I process and retain text at a much faster pace if it's read aloud as well—especially when I'm stressed. But Cameron, the lucky bastard he is, graduated last term and is eagerly starting his new life in Seattle. I wish him the best, but he picked one heck of a time to up and move away. We had a great system and I've been able to pull top grades—he not only helped with reading, but he talked me through my thoughts before I wrote each of my papers.

I'm hoping I won't need a tutor. There's only one class, in particular, I'll require assistance with this term—psychology. I've spread out my heavy reading courses over the last three years keeping my load manageable—but somehow this class was missed. I need this course and another psychology class, to graduate. With it only being offered this semester, I can't put it off.

I've spent days working on this paper. I think I managed my time well, but after a while, the statistics and specific facts may have gotten the better of me. I guess I laid my cards on the table, and the chips will fall where they may. But if things go the way I fear, I won't have time to waiver. I'll need to suck up my pride by reaching out to the learning center for support. Hopefully, I can meet with a new tutor sooner than later.

"Hey, Z, what's up?" comes from a familiar voice, causing me to stop in my tracks.

It doesn't take long to place the greeting from DeShawn. Together, we stand a full head taller than most of the students on campus here at Columbia River University. He and I have been playing ball together since freshman year. Over the last three years, he's also become one of my closest friends on the team. He, Grey, Drew, Tre, and I make up the starting five at CRU. We have to be in sync both on and off the court if we want another championship this season. There's almost nothing I won't do for this man, so of course, I stop and greet him.

"Hey, man. I'm off to class over in Deacon Hall. You're welcome to walk with me, but we gotta keep movin'."

Nodding, DeShawn grins. "I'm heading that way. What time are you done today?"

"I've got class until three. Then I'm meeting with a trainer to work on keeping my shoulder up when I shoot from my non-dominant hand."

Nodding, DeShawn grins. "Alright. We need you in top shape if we're gonna get CRU another championship this season."

"That's the plan." I won't say more than that, as I'm not about to jinx us. The eyes of the nation are waiting to see how we'll come back after that amazing win last season and I prefer to just focus on one game at a time as we make our way through this season.

"Grey and I are grabbing dinner at the Thai restaurant next to campus, wanna join us?"

"Where's Drew?" I ask of their other roommate. Those three are usually thick as thieves.

DeShawn shrugs as if I should know. "He's studying—what do you expect?"

Drew's been applying to med schools all around the country and we're all proud of him. But that doesn't mean we don't throw shade his way to give him a hard time. "Should've known. I'd rather stop by your place for his cookin' but if he's busy, I guess Thai will work."

No joke, if Drew wasn't set on being a doctor, the man should open his own restaurant. I'd gladly eat at his place over any restaurant in town. But I'd rather hang with my boys than eat in the dining hall on campus, despite the fact that athletes get one heck of a meal plan.

When we arrive at Deacon Hall, I nod in the direction of my class. "I'll text you when I'm done with the trainer."

"Sounds good, man. See ya then."

And with that, I take the stairs two at a time rushing into the building. I land in my seat and press record on my audio device just as Professor Easton begins her lecture. Though I'd prefer the back of the room, I typically sit up front to get better sound quality when I review lectures later.

As she begins her lecture about a case of a woman with factitious disorder imposed by another or FDIA as she calls it —she explains that it was formerly called Munchausen syndrome by proxy. I'm disgusted that an innocent child was abused in such a way to gain attention for their guardian. There is zero excuse for child abuse, and hearing about this case makes my gut roil. I doubt I'll have to listen to this lecture again as it's seared into my memory. I seriously don't understand how people like this can keep their children. I'm so engrossed in our class discussion, the hour passes by before I know it.

Just as it's about to end, the professor announces, "I've got your latest papers. Once you receive it, you're welcome to leave. Remember my office hours are on Tuesdays and

Thursdays at two. Stop by or drop me a message and I'll be happy to discuss any concerns you may have."

I watch as she and her TA pass out the papers. Eventually, mine lands on my desk face-down as Professor Easton grimaces.

This can't be a good sign.

Sighing heavily, I know the best course of action is to just rip off the Band-Aid.

Sure enough—there on the top of the page in bright blue ink is a large D.

This just won't do.

But I have no one to blame but myself.

It's time to put my pride aside and ask the coach who's set me up before for help. Hopefully, someone can fit my busy schedule into theirs. With the semester already underway, I just hope I'm not too late.

2

———

ARI

LEARNING CTR: Zander Williams will meet you at the main campus library at 8:00 a.m. Saturday morning and study room 3-B has been reserved. Let me know if you have any questions. – Tamara

I'm not sure how many times I've read this text. When I agreed to work from eight to five each weekend, I never in my wildest dreams thought I'd be taken up on the offer. I mean, what college student in their right mind gets up this early to study on a Saturday? Thank goodness I didn't go home this weekend because I can really use the extra cash from this last-minute add to my schedule. My best friend's getting married and we're taking a girls' trip later this month before her big day.

Zander Williams.

The world must be playing a cruel joke on me.

There must be another Zander Williams on campus, right?

This can't be the star basketball player who's hot as sin but has a reputation for being a player both on and off the court.

There's no way he would need my help.

Sure, I'm a fan of basketball. I also happen to know most of the team's stats because I'm typically the scorekeeper at home games. Not only do I get court-side seats, but it keeps me involved in a game I love. I play basketball myself, but I'm by no means good enough for a D-1 school, so I've joined a rec league here on campus.

I'm a fan of his game on the court, though not of him personally. Until recently, I've been in a long-term relationship so I've never dealt with him on a personal level, but I've watched plenty from the sidelines as he's gone through a gaggle of women over his three years here at Columbia River. Don't get me started on the pranks he and his buddies pull on one another. Thank God, I've never let myself get close enough to be the butt of one of their jokes.

Glancing at my clock, I'm disappointed to find my time is running out on my peaceful morning. I've got twenty minutes to drive on campus and be at the library. Normally, I'd walk but it's a damp and dreary spring day in the Pacific Northwest, so instead I'll just park in the underground garage. Sighing, I dump what's left of my coffee in the sink, then quickly rinse my cup and place it in the dishwasher. I've already had my quota and I'm just not feeling it today.

With eight minutes to spare, I easily spot Zander already waiting just under the overhang of the building staying out of the rain. Being six-seven, he stands out in any crowd, but as the campus is deserted at this hour, he's the only one in sight. His face is buried in his phone, so I use this opportunity to take him in.

He's wearing long black athletic pants that fit his sculpted muscles perfectly. I've seen him enough times to know what he's got hiding underneath. He's also wearing an oversized CRU sweatshirt and sneakers similar to what the players wear off the court after practices.

When I stop right in front of him, he looks up from his phone and grins.

Before he can utter a word, I quickly introduce myself. "Hi, Zander, I'm Ari. Has the library opened yet?"

"Ari?" Zander's jaw drops as he looks me up and down. Not in an, *I'm checking you out* way, but more out of confusion.

"Yes?"

Suddenly he shakes his head and stands to his full height. "Sorry. Coach said a guy was meeting me this morning and I wasn't expecting... well, you."

Cocking my head to the side, I meet his eyes. "Will that be a problem?"

Zander visibly appears as if he's backpedaling and if I wasn't slightly annoyed by his question, I'd almost laugh at how his expression morphs from confused to quickly sputtering, "No... not at all. That's what I get for making assumptions. I... uh have no problem with you being my tutor, I was just expecting a dude. All I was given is your first name and since my last tutor was... well... that's not the point. The point is I'm sorry I mistook you for someone else. That's totally on me."

Huh. That's unexpected.

"Well, I'm Ariadne—but I'll only ever answer to Ari as no one ever pronounces my given name right. My mom was a huge Greek mythology buff. She met my dad during a semester abroad in London and with their love of literature— whelp, here I am."

"Is your dad British?"

"Nope. He's actually from Tunisia. He was there on business and when Mom's visa expired, they relocated here."

Geez... why did I just give him my entire backstory?

Slowly Zander says, "Ar-ree-ad-nee. That's not so hard. It's a beautiful name and it suits you."

Why did the way his lips curl at the end make my belly flip?

Nope. Shut this down. You've already said too much.

Jutting out my chin to prove a point, I quickly speak before what-ever-the-hell I was feeling just then can have any merit. "Well, it's Ari – like Are-ree. No need to worry about my given name. I'm only called Ariadne by solicitors and when I'm in trouble so let's stick with Ari, got it?"

With a quick nod of his head, his smile disappears. "Got it." Then he turns to the door when the distinct sound of the bar unlocks. "You ready to get started?" Leaning in, he reaches for the handle and opens it for me and I walk through it.

Wordlessly, I walk into the library and head straight to the study rooms. I'm familiar with room 3-B, but the moment Zander enters the room with me, it's suddenly much smaller than I remember. The ventilation must not be working either as the room fills with his scent and it's all I can do to focus on the task at hand.

As he sits in the middle of one side of the long wooden table, I quickly walk around to sit across from him. There's a total of six chairs around this table as it's a room meant for groups. By the time I grab my laptop and notebook, I find Zander has his notebooks, voice recorder, and laptop out as well.

Just as I place my pen on my notebook, Zander's deep voice fills the room as his dark brown eyes pin mine in place. "So that we don't waste anyone's time, why don't I tell you what I'll need help with the most. You see, I have dyslexia. I can read and write, but my processing speed when I'm stressed out slows down even further than usual. I typically record lectures as well as my study sessions with my tutor, so I can go back and listen to everything before assignments as well as assessments. Do you mind if I turn this on?" He points to his digital voice recorder.

"No. Go ahead."

Smiling, he continues, "Thanks. Since freshman year, I've had the same tutor. We had a system that kept me on top of my grades and sometimes even at the top of my classes."

Cautiously, I ask, "What did that entail?"

"Honestly, my working memory kicks ass. If I can hear things once, I typically remember it. But when I'm stressed—which let's face it I am—during basketball season, it takes me longer to read and retain information. I'm not dumb. But I'm man enough to know I need help from time to time, too."

Zander's bluntness about his disability tugs at my heartstrings and I wonder if I've misjudged him.

"What exactly do you need me to help you with? Is it the content for your psychology class or something else?"

Zander's long intake of breath is all that can be heard as he leans forward, placing his elbows on the table, and steeples his fingers in front of his mouth in a fist. "Look, like I said. This isn't something I spend a lot of time talking about but I've got a game later today and I need to get my focus on *that,* sooner than later. By the way, thanks again for meeting with me on such short notice. If you don't mind my schedule is a little chaotic, so hopefully we'll find times that work for both of us."

"That still doesn't answer my question. What exactly do you need... from me?"

Rolling his eyes, his lips form a small grin, then he exhales heavily. "In the past here's what's worked. I'm good with any content that's already in digital form and lectures as I record them. What I need help with is having someone read the additional text assigned that isn't already in digital format. It also helps when someone walks me through my assignments and helps formulate my thoughts before I complete them. I thought I could do it on my own, but this D on my first paper proved otherwise," he says as he points at his closed folder. "I can't have grades like this and play. Thankfully, I aced the quiz last week so my overall grade isn't in the toilet, but I must do better."

"That seems easy enough. Where should we start today?"

He pulls out his course syllabus along with two articles that he's already printed. I take a moment to familiarize myself with them. I haven't worked with this professor in particular, but as I took the class last year, I'm confident I can help.

"Okay, let's start by going over what your next assignment is, then I'll read these case studies before we leave."

"I'd like to say I'm not usually in such a rush, but I won't lie to you. I'm due at the coliseum in less than two hours and I'm not sure how far we'll get. Would you mind giving me your number so we can meet up another day as well? I need to nail this so I can make up for my idiotic attempt last week."

Zander's no-nonsense approach to his studies is a breath of fresh air. Typically, I get involved once a student is severely behind and pride gets in their way, so every excuse known to man as to why they're behind in the first place is made. I respect his proactive stance and I'm eager to help.

"I think that can be arranged."

We spend the next twenty minutes going over the expectations for his next paper. Not only is it a ten-page paper, but his sources won't easily be found in audio format—as it's centered around case studies from years ago. It involves a group of children and their biological basis of human social behavior—which essentially means his paper is about the start of developmental psychology. In our limited time, we get through one article and we discuss how he can use it in his paper.

When I realize the next article is over twenty pages long, I quickly suggest meeting again. "I'm not sure we'll get through this one and get you to your game on time. I'm free in the morning if you're available. Then we can give this all the time it deserves."

"I've got a workout with the guys, but I'll have time

afterward. I typically spend Sundays studying. Wanna meet here again?"

"The library doesn't open until noon, but I'm only available until three." *I've got a fitting for my bridesmaid dress at four. We should be done by then.*

"Noon works for me. Thanks," he says on a nod as he gathers his papers. "I don't mean to cut this short, but if I don't get my head in my game soon, coach will have my ass." Standing he stops to look me in the eye. "I mean it, Ari, thank you. I really couldn't do this without you."

I nod in understanding, still dumbfounded, and in awe of Zander's bluntness. The way his eyes pin mine, I easily get caught up in them. He may come off cocky and arrogant, but now that I'm getting to know him, I'm fairly certain I've misjudged him.

Just as he reaches the door, my manners kick in. "Good luck today."

Stopping in his tracks, his head swivels as a grin spreads across his face. "I'll take all the luck I can get. Thanks again, Ari. See you tomorrow."

THE TEAM HAS BEEN on fire since the game started. Energy radiates through the coliseum as CRU stacks points on the board. The Huskies are giving us a run for our money, but each and every time they pull ahead, CRU comes back with a vengeance. The boys are in sync and it's beyond beautiful to watch.

From the moment Zander entered the court for warm-ups, he's held my attention. Maybe it's because I spent time with him earlier today, but I'm not sure there's a move he's made yet that I haven't been aware of.

Which is crazy.

I mean, I've never paid him any attention before, so why is he all I can think about now?

I'm brought out of my revelry when Zander suddenly steals the ball and makes a fast break for the net. Number forty stays hot on his trail and almost tips the ball as Zander pulls up short and lands a perfect jump shot instead of the expected lay-up.

The crowd roars, and for a fleeting second, I see a quick smile with a nod of his head in celebration. But that's all. The moment the ball is thrown in and back in play, he's focused on his next move as he sprints down the court.

The man is in his zone.

Zander's by far not the leading scorer for this game, as Drew is crushing it. But his points come when they matter most. Besides, there's no stopping him when he makes a break for it.

When the final buzzer sounds, the walls shake with the enthusiasm of the crowd as the announcer booms, "And just like that, Columbia River University has done it again!"

What he doesn't say is that we're one step closer to the division title.

Not one student will speak that thought aloud. We're proud of our team, but we refuse to jinx them either. It's a long road to even make it into the sweet sixteen. Nope—our team takes it one game at a time, as they keep their focus on beating our next opponent.

After fist-bumping Aaron, the official timekeeper, I put away the equipment the best I can, then gather my things to leave. By the time I'm done, the players are in locker rooms and the stands have cleared out.

Even though I spent the entire game at center court and Zander passed me several times, not once did he notice me. He nodded once to Aaron when he was subbed back in during the first part of the second half, but I may as well have been invisible.

Is he really that arrogant, or was his attention so focused on the game that he truly didn't see me?

3

———

ZANDER

OKAY, I'll admit—I was wrong.

I'd thought Cameron and I were in sync, but he has nothing on Ari.

Due to her flexibility and brilliance, she and I have met for the last two days, which puts me ahead of schedule for my next paper. I hate feeling behind and we've created a system which should keep me on track. After explaining in detail my thoughts about the assignment and what I wanted to include, we worked efficiently in finding sources in support of my argument.

I'll admit, I may have given her shit when she pulled out her collection of highlighters, but they've totally come in handy when I needed to cite a specific article last night, while writing. Since I record all sessions to review if I get stuck, I love that she's even been thoughtful enough to mention the importance of each color of highlighted information orally before she highlights it on the cheat sheet she made with the specific topic I plan to include on my paper. I've been doing this for years and this simple step never even crossed my mind.

I'll admit I used to view my tutor sessions as a dutiful chore to check off a list, but time with Ari passes with ease and I find myself eager to show up again the next day. Not only does she get my drive to succeed, but I'd be blind if I didn't notice how her beautiful smile lights up the room when she lets her armor slip and sense of humor shine through.

Ari's a tough nut to crack. I'm sure there's more to her than the straitlaced studious side she shows. After our study sessions, my thoughts linger on my tutor much longer than I want to admit.

"Hey, Z, great game," a guy says as I enter the library, changing my focus to him.

Nodding in agreement, I grin but keep my pace so I'm not late to meet Ari. "Thanks, man. It was a team effort. Drew's on fire these days."

He can see I'm on a mission but it doesn't stop him from saying, "I can't wait to see you light up the court against Oregon tonight. Knock 'em dead."

This makes me grin. "I'll do my best." I chuckle as I reach for the handle on our designated study room. I don't give him a chance to respond before I slip inside and shut the door. To my surprise, the room isn't empty.

I pride myself on being early, but even being twenty minutes ahead of schedule, Ari's already here. Her books are sprawled out on the table and her head pops up in surprise at my abrupt entrance.

Looking from her to the door, I wonder if she's expecting another client. "Am I... interrupting?"

Gathering her things, she quickly spouts, "Nope, not at all. I had time between sessions and I thought I'd write my own paper."

Glancing at my watch. "Well, don't let me interrupt you. I've got some things I can work on."

"Don't be silly, Zander. You're here. There's a game tonight and even though it's hours away, I'm sure you'd rather check this project off your list."

This is the first she's mentioned basketball, so I'm caught off guard. "You watch?"

Looking back at her work, she shrugs. "I have from time to time."

There's something about the way she says it so dismissively that gives me pause. In my short time with her, I know without a doubt, she's not a jersey chaser. She's never been phased by my status on campus, but her casual mention of watching the game tells me there might be more to her story.

Before I can confirm my gut feeling, she asks, "How far did you get on your paper yesterday?"

Waggling my brows, I puff out my chest. "I think I'm just about finished. I'll read through it again to make sure I didn't miss anything."

"Really?" Ari's genuine smile is infectious and I find myself mirroring her expression with pride. "Hand it over and I'll take a look."

Grabbing my folder, I proudly hand over my ten-page

paper and tease, "Here you go. Highlight the crap out of it. I'm sure there's plenty of room for improvements."

Shaking her head, she says, "It won't be that bad."

"Seriously, all joking aside. If you see anything wrong, I need to know. Here's the rubric. I can't afford anything less than an A after bombing the last one."

Nodding, she takes my paper and wordlessly begins reading.

Somehow the silence as she reads isn't awkward. Getting out my laptop, I pull up the document ready for any changes she'll suggest. Eventually, she reaches for a blue highlighter in her bag of pens and marks a sentence, and a page or so later, she does it again.

It practically kills me to practice patience and not have immediate feedback. Though in my short time with Ari, I've learned it's best to let her get her thoughts complete and not interrupt her. If it's anything like yesterday, it's probably grammatical errors, rather than content.

As I've written this paper over the past few days, my text-to-speech app has gotten a workout. I'm fairly certain I've nailed the content, but having her look it over will give me peace of mind. She read the first few pages as we worked on that yesterday, then I went home and knocked the rest out last night. I'm eager to check this off my lengthy to-do list.

Unlike most of my teammates, I live in a one-bedroom apartment on campus. I need time to recharge my social battery at the end of the day. I also require less distractions than most, so I can listen and complete my assignments aloud. I love my friends and teammates; however, one year of living with them was more than enough. I barely made it through my required stint freshman year. I was lucky I didn't land on academic probation because I simply couldn't concentrate.

After hearing about my academic needs, Coach B. helped me realize dyslexia doesn't define me. He not only set me up with Cameron as my tutor, but helped me find a place on campus where I could study and thrive academically. I swear Coach Bradford was a game changer for me in more ways than one, since arriving at CRU.

Ari breaks me out of my thoughts with a low sigh as she leans back in her chair. "I think you've got it. I've highlighted a few things that could be tightened up, as well as some typos. Overall it sounds good."

We spend the next few minutes reviewing her notes, then I save my document once more. With that task complete, I pull out today's assignment and grin hopefully. "Since we still have time, do you mind reading an article I was assigned today?"

"That's what I'm here for. I'd hate to get behind after all this hard work."

A low laugh escapes before I can contain it. "No kidding."

When we finish, our time is up. Quickly we gather our things and walk out of the study room together. Just as we make it to the outer doors of the library, she suddenly turns in my direction causing me to pause.

"Good luck in your game tonight, Zander."

"Thanks." I nod in appreciation, holding the door for her.

Once outside, it's obvious we're parting ways. But she stops abruptly once again.

"Uh... don't take this the wrong way... but you're dropping

your left shoulder when you take a shot from the left side of the court with your non-dominant hand. It's why your stats aren't as strong when you drive left. So... keep your shoulder up—or stick with your dominant hand."

Holy shit—this girl does way more than watch an occasional game. I've spent the last week or so working with the trainer on this exact problem. Only a real fan would know this particular detail though. She definitely watches more than the occasional game.

As I stare in disbelief with my jaw hanging on the ground she simply shrugs. "I just thought you'd want to know."

When my mouth catches up to my brain she's over ten paces away. "Will you be at tonight's game?"

Chuckling, she shakes her head. "I haven't missed one since freshman year. Look, I gotta run, or I'll be late to my next gig. Keep that elbow up. I'll be watching. Oh, and good luck tonight!"

Holy hell. This girl knows her way around the court.

How have I not seen her at games before?

4

ARI

I'VE BEEN KICKING myself for my comment since leaving Zander this afternoon. Normally I'd never insert myself into another player's headspace—especially before a big game. But his coaches must be working with him on that skill, or they aren't worth a penny they're being paid. We have a top-notch coaching staff at CRU and I'm sure it's already on their radar, especially if I'm noticing it from the sidelines.

Hopefully, he knows I meant no harm by it. CRU can't afford for anyone to be off their game—especially Zander. He provides nearly as many assists as points on the board.

By the time Zander's due to arrive on court, I've worked myself up over this internal dilemma. Now, my stomach is tight and my nerves are completely fried.

Why the hell did I mention it?

My stomach flips when Zander's the first to enter the court before the scheduled pre-game team warm-ups. His gait is casual and instead of focusing on the ball in his hand, his head slowly swivels around at the crowd. It's early and the seats are only starting to fill, so I shouldn't be surprised when his eyes lock on mine.

Even from across the court, I feel the impact of the playful smirk deep in my belly. The man has a beautiful smile. My heart rate spikes as he rolls his eyes and jogs in my direction.

What the hell is he doing?

He never talks to anyone before games.

Shit. Maybe I've messed with his game.

The sound of my heartbeat is louder than the thumping music as my pulse rockets through my ears. It only increases when he stops right in front of me. He just stares—as he rolls the right side of his lower lip under his teeth, my breath hitches.

What the hell is he thinking?

Is it possible to die from the unknown?

Finally, after what feels like an eternity he points to my chair, then the scoreboard and asks, "Do you do this at every game?"

Not knowing what to say, I just nod.

"Seriously?" he asks in disbelief. "How have I not seen you?"

I pointedly remind him. "You're usually focused on your game." Which is what he should be doing—now. Crap. I really shouldn't have said anything.

Before he can say anything else, the buzzer goes off and his team rushes onto the court for their pre-game warm-ups.

Zander glances to the court, then back at me. Shaking his head, he knows this isn't the time to talk. Raising a brow in challenge he quickly adds, "This conversation isn't over," before running toward his teammates.

What the hell could he possibly want to talk about?

As he warms up, I watch his every move.

Of course, I've got nothing but time and my keen ability to overthink those four little words. He never spares me a second glance once he's out on the court. The next thing I know, he runs to the locker room with the rest of his team, and when he returns, the MC announces each player.

Thankfully, once the game starts, I'm distracted enough not to remain stuck in my head. Otherwise, I'd likely march on to the court, rip his arms off, and efficiently beat him with them for getting me so worked up.

I hate uncertainty.

It isn't that he wants to finish our conversation, but the arrogant way he told me we weren't finished. His expression was unreadable. I still have no freaking clue what he is thinking, which is beyond annoying.

Thankfully, Zander's performance has been top-notch and he hasn't dropped his shoulder once in the first half, so I must not have rattled him. My heart races as I watch him pass the ball to Grey Gibbons just in time to drop a three-pointer at the buzzer. I'm on my feet in an instant cheering along with the crowd. By the time the team runs off the court at half-time, we're up by eighteen and another win is on the horizon.

The boys are fierce when they return. Oregon gives it their best, but they're no match for Columbia River in the end. The final score is 91 to 78 and I'm beaming with pride for CRU. I cheer as Zander jumps and chest bumps both Grey and

DeShawn before making his rounds to the other members of the team. Tre Madison, another senior from the team, is the last to celebrate with Zander with an elaborate handshake, before pulling each other in to pat the other on the back the way men do. It is a sight to behold to watch history in the making. I love witnessing their dreams come true from the sidelines.

"You want some help packing up your things?" Aaron says, pulling me back to reality.

Forcing my eyes from Zander, I turn with a shrug. "Nah, I've got it. But thanks." When I'm done, Zander's nowhere in sight. Surely, he doesn't expect me to wait around for him. The team always goes into the locker room and some players are even selected to talk with the press afterward. From what I've seen on the highlight reels, Zander often participates. I'm sure he's got much better things on his mind than satisfying my curiosity.

With a heavy sigh, I make my way out of the coliseum, wondering what tomorrow will bring.

I WISH I could say my nerves had calmed down before our next tutoring session, but they haven't. Of course, as an overthinker and with nothing but time on my hands, I've imagined every possible scenario for how we might *finish* our conversation.

Why couldn't I have just kept my mouth shut?

I'm startled when the door suddenly swings open and

Zander's larger-than-life personality fills the room. His grin is triumphant and his chest puffs out as he exclaims, "You'll never believe what happened today, Ari!" His boisterous mood is infectious and I'd be a liar if I didn't admit that his beautiful grin makes my skin tingle.

Trying to match his jovial tone, I play along. "What's that, Zander?"

"This!" he shouts as he pulls out a packet of paper from behind his back, then throws it on the table so that it smoothly slides right in front of me.

It takes me a second to process what I'm seeing. But by the time I do, I find him grinning triumphantly beside me, reaching for my hand. "Thank you so much! I couldn't have done this without you," he gushes out as he pulls me into the biggest bear hug imaginable. My feet dangle in the air.

When my brain finally catches up to what's happening, I'm enveloped by his rich musky scent. Damn, this man smells amazing. I find myself returning his hug with the same level of intensity. "It was all you, Zander."

He sets me down and briefly rocks me from side to side before stepping back to place his large hands on my shoulders. "Seriously, Ari. I am so thankful you're my tutor. Your help has been invaluable. I truly wouldn't have aced this without you."

For a short moment, he just stares into my eyes as if he doesn't think his message has sunk in yet. But what he doesn't understand is that I was just a tool. He did the work on his own and he earned this. "All you needed was help accessing the text. You're the one who earned this A. I hope you know that."

His beautiful lips pull into a smug grin as he waggles his brows. "Well, I for one think we make an excellent team!" Reaching out a fist, he waits for me to bump mine with his.

"Okay, okay," I concede when I return his fist bump. "I guess I'll take the assist. But you're the one who made the shot."

"Speaking of shots..." His lips pull to the side and his brows raise. His expression would almost be adorable if my stomach didn't lurch from the reminder of our last conversation. The knot tightens when he adds, "I have a bone to pick with you."

Oh, shit. Why did I have to put my two cents in where it didn't belong?

5

———

ZANDER

FOR A SPLIT SECOND, I watch as an array of emotions flit across Ari's face and I can't decipher their meaning. Then her chin juts out with confidence as her arms cross over her chest. "Oh, really, why's that?"

From the little I know of her, she won't back down from a challenge.

To lighten the mood, I cock a brow in her direction. Though instead of remaining toe-to-toe in challenge I step back to my usual side of the table and take a seat. But of course, my mouth won't let it go.

"What was your plan? To keep giving me pointers until I pulled my head out of my ass and finally noticed you?"

Shrugging, she smirks. "Maybe."

"I don't know how I didn't notice you before. Seriously, Ari, I feel like an ass."

"You have no reason to."

Taking a moment to gather my thoughts, I exhale heavily

then admit, "You probably think I'm a pompous, arrogant jerk."

She shakes her head. "Not at all, actually."

"How can you not? I'm either the most obtuse man on the planet..."

"Or you're the most focused." She smiles with a casual shrug as if it should explain everything. "Now that I've gotten to know you better these past few weeks, I'd likely go with that, though before... let's just say, I might've agreed with you... but now—I know without a doubt, you're anything but arrogant."

My mouth hangs open as I process her words. We've played a few home games since Ari's become my tutor. If she's been there and I haven't noticed her, how can she not consider me a self-absorbed asshat?

She's partially right—I am extremely focused when I'm on the court. But not noticing the scorekeeper? Especially one as beautiful as her, that's a whole other world of jack-assery. I really need to check myself.

"Oh, stop." She swats at the air. "Whatever you're thinking in that big ole' head of yours, give yourself a break. You work your ass off on that court. The only way you get to the level you are at is to get in the zone and eliminate all distractions. Like I said, I've been to every home game since our freshman year. I know for a fact that you hardly notice anything that isn't on the court when you're playing—so don't get your nose out of joint because you didn't notice a little nobody like me."

"First, I'd hardly say you're a nobody," I counter, but her phone chimes before I can continue.

"Crap. I thought I'd put that on vibrate." But when her

eyes dart to the incoming text, they light up and she gasps. "Mind if I check this? It's from my best friend who's getting married in two weeks. Hopefully, our plans for this weekend haven't changed."

Leaning back in my chair, I shrug. "Not at all."

"Thanks." She grins, swiping open her phone.

She suddenly gasps, then her entire demeanor changes. I find my heart rate accelerating in anticipation of bad news.

As her lower lip rolls under her teeth, her eyes begin blinking rapidly.

"What's going on?" I finally ask when I can't take the unknown any longer.

"It's... uh..." She looks to the ceiling and blinks a few more times as if she's holding back tears, before adding the word "Nothing."

I'm obviously not the sharpest tool in the shed, but I do know a thing or two about women. The way she's frantically blinking and her quick use of the word *nothing*, I know she's anything but okay. She's fucking holding back tears as she pretends all is good—but that shit doesn't fly with me.

"Sell that to someone else," comes out rougher than I intend. "What's going on? Is your friend okay? You can't go from jovial to distressed in a nanosecond and tell me *nothing's* wrong."

Sighing heavily, she looks to the ceiling for a long moment before meeting my eyes. "Sasha, my best friend in the entire world, is getting married in two weeks. I truly couldn't be happier for her. Apparently, my ex is bringing his new girlfriend and she's giving me a heads up."

"Why will your ex be at your best friend's wedding?" I ask with interest. Most people cut ties once they split, so why is he showing up?

"Because he's her fiancé's brother. Dylan and I set them up on a blind date—and the rest is history. I promised her I wouldn't let it be weird when he and I broke up."

"You're a bigger person than I," I admit.

"Sasha's been my best friend since kindergarten. There's nothing I won't do for her. Including being in the room with my ex and the one he cheated with. I'm her maid of honor and I'd never bail on her—even if the asshole-of-the-year attends."

"When's the wedding?" I ask, pulling out my phone.

"The weekend after next," she says, wrapping her arms around herself.

"Is this a black-tie event, or will a regular suit do?" I ask casually, pulling up my calendar app—yep, just what I thought; it's our game-free weekend.

Her brows knit together at my question and I can't help but grin. She's one of the smartest people I know, but in this moment, she's clueless and frankly it's adorable.

"Uh, I'm sure only the groomsmen will be in tuxes, but why are you asking?"

Ignoring her, I ask a more pressing question, hoping like hell it's local. "Where's the wedding?" I'm free so I can drive just about anywhere, but I can't swing airline tickets with this short of notice.

"Seaside, Oregon.... Why on Earth are you grinning?"

"I'm sure Sasha will understand your sudden need to bring a plus one."

Now it's her turn to be shocked. "Who?"

"I'm free, I have a suit, and I'll be your date." When her mouth drops open, I tease, "You'd better watch out, you'll catch flies with that mouth of yours if you keep staring at me like that."

"But... I.... But... why?" she sputters.

I've either just stepped in it—big time, or this is the most brilliant idea I've ever had. Of course, the jury's still out. Somehow, I feel triumphant as she tilts her head to the side and studies me carefully.

"Why not?" I counter and wait for a lengthy list of excuses. "I happen to have excellent dancing skills *and* I can pull off the doting boyfriend perfectly." Placing a hand over my chest, I give her my best angelic expression.

"Um... why would you bother?"

Ugh... this woman.

"Again.... Why not? From the look on your face, things obviously didn't end well with your ex, and let's be clear that was his loss."

And apparently, Ari's officially tongue-tied, which would be hysterical if I wasn't trying to convince her of something important.

I wait patiently as her mouth morphs from a firm line to a wide O, then back to a grimace.

When I can't take the silence any longer, I hedge, "Do you have any better offers?"

Her brows knit together as she sputters, "Well... uh... I mean, no."

"Fine, it's settled. I'm available any time after the game on

Thursday evening, but I do have to be back early Sunday morning. Will that work for you?"

"Uh... I have a brunch on Sunday."

"When are you leaving for Seaside?"

For some reason, this simple question makes her cringe and suck in a breath. "Thursday evening. I have to help Sasha with decorations on Friday before the rehearsal dinner."

"Will this ex of yours be at the rehearsal dinner?"

Sighing heavily, she groans. "Unfortunately."

"Just tell me when and where you want me, and I'll be there" comes out before I can think better of it. I totally owe her a solid after all the help she's been to me these past few weeks. This is the least I can do.

She studies me carefully then asks, "You really want to drive *all the way* to Seaside?"

"I will if you want me there. Besides, it's only two hours away. It's not like I'd be driving all day or anything."

It's almost comical to watch her wheels spin.

"But... where will you stay?"

"You let me figure that out."

"Zander," she says on a warning.

"What? Your job is to worry about making Sasha's wedding memorable. My job is being the doting date that's enamored by you. I'm available Friday afternoon, so if you want help decorating, I'll be there."

She slowly reaches out to poke my arm with her index finger as she asks, "Are you for real?"

This time, I do lose a bit of control and a chuckle escapes.

I can't help it. She's adorable.

"Yep. I'm as real as they come. What do you say? I can arrive Friday and stay through the wedding?"

"But what will you do Saturday morning? Sasha and I will be busy at the spa, getting our hair and makeup done."

"Have you been to Seaside? There's plenty to do—even in the winter. I can occupy myself, trust me. It'll be great getting away from campus for the day, so this is a win for me, too."

Cocking her head to the side, she finally meets my gaze. "If you're sure… then yes. I'd love to have you there as support. But if you need me to split the cost of anything, just ask."

"Did you hear the part that I get a break? I'm good." There's no way I'd let her pay, even if I have to dip into my savings. Things like this are why I work my ass off in the summer.

Grabbing a seat from the table, I pull it out for her. "Now… if you're ready, let's get this study session over with so I can be at my training session on time this evening. I've got a shoulder that keeps slipping and I must break that habit."

Palming her face, Ari shakes her head. "Will I ever hear the end of that?"

"Someday, you're gonna tell me how you even noticed *that* little tidbit. But today is not that day. Remember, I've got a mind like an elephant and I'll seek out information in the near future. I don't mean to be a total taskmaster, but I really do have a meeting in a little over an hour and I could use the help with reading the article assigned today."

Quickly, I dig into my backpack and retrieve my assignment.

As soon as I lay it on the table, she asks, "Are you always this way?"

"Focused? Yes. But you already knew that."

Shaking her head, I see a grin pull at her lips. "You know there's a fine line between focused and bossy, right?"

Christ, I guess I did go all bull in a China shop with her. Sighing heavily, I admit my truth. "I never want to force you into something you don't want, but I'm also known for cutting to the chase and getting it done, too. If I'm too pushy, I give you permission to push right back, got it?"

Grinning, she reaches for the packet of paper I've set out on the table. "I can totally work with that, Zander. Now let's get to work; you're showing improvement with that arm, but I don't want to be blamed if you let it slip again."

"Now you're just being mean." I grin and she knows I'm nowhere near offended.

6

ZANDER

IT'S BEEN a hell of a week and we just about got our asses handed to us against Seattle, but luckily Tre and Drew were able to pull off a few lucky shots and brought us a victory at the end. Now, we're back on the bus for the three-hour drive back to campus. We have another game tomorrow night, then we're free for the weekend.

It's late and the lights on the bus are dim but many of us are still wide awake and buzzing with energy after pulling off this win. Some of us are glued to our phones, while others hold quiet conversations with our seat mates.

DeShawn plopped himself down next to me as I took the window seat. He's been texting someone ever since. Giving him some privacy, I've been zoning out the window. My phone holds no interest for me as everyone I'd be texting is either on the bus or in a different time zone, as I'm originally from Michigan.

Eventually, DeShawn bumps my arm to get my attention

as he stows his phone in his pocket. "Got any plans for our free weekend, Z? Some of the guys are talkin' about getting together."

"I'd love to, but I gotta pass."

"What? Since when do you have better things to do?" I know he's only teasing, but I can tell by the look in his eye, I've piqued his curiosity.

Rubbing the bridge of my nose, I admit, "I've got a weddin' in Seaside."

Obviously, this is the last thing he expects because his eyes bug out as his voice raises. "Who do we know that's getting married?"

"Calm down, D. You don't know 'em. I'm going with my tutor, Ari."

DeShawn's face practically splits in half. "Ah, so that's how it is... your tutor."

Playfully, I shove his arm and hopefully his thoughts away. "Naw, it's not like that."

And the jackass he is mocks me with an exaggerated nod of his head as he draws out, "Sure it isn't."

"Seriously, man, I'm just doing her a favor. She'd just found out her ex and the girl he cheated on her with are showing up. He's the brother of the groom, so she can't avoid him."

"Ouch. That's gotta hurt."

"No kidding. I can't let her go through that alone. Ari's been a godsend since Cameron graduated last semester. You know how my dyslexia kicks in when I'm under pressure. Seriously, I'm just helping her out."

DeShawn chuckles once, then smirks in Drew's direction diagonally from us. "I'm still not buying this—I'm only doing it for my tutor thing. Have you *seen* Drew lately?"

What the hell is he talking about?

"What does Drew have to do with this?" I eventually ask when he stares at me as if I'm missing something.

Clearly, I'm not connecting the dots.

"Oh, you haven't heard that Dr. Drew has a thing for his lab partner?"

Everyone knows Drew is using his skills on the court to pay his way through undergrad, so he can get into med school. He is adamant about not dating during the season. I mean, the man is more focused than anyone on the team when it comes to keeping his eye on his goals. Clearly, I didn't hear DeShawn right, so as I look at Drew wildly texting from across the aisle, I whisper, "What do you mean?"

DeShawn rolls his eyes and chuckles loud enough so that only I can hear. "Oh, it was classic. You know how group projects can be with others on campus since we won last year? Well, apparently, Drew found one of the few girls on campus that didn't recognize him. He was convinced he'd found the perfect partner. Then when she showed up to study a few weeks ago, apparently she blew his mind."

"What do you mean? She pulled a bait and switch?"

"Not even close. She had no idea why everyone kept talking to him in class or while they were in public. But something must have happened after she came over to our place to study because suddenly the guy spends way more time texting than ever before. Don't even get me started on the dopey perma-grin plastered to his face. He's even inviting her over for dinner."

"Well, the man can cook," I admit, rubbing my stomach. "That's a great angle."

"No, man, look at him. This is way more than just some girl. He may be too smart to realize it. But whoever this girl is, I think the mighty Dr. Drew has fallen... hard."

"Has he said it's serious?" I ask in wonder. Just watching him smile like that at his phone, the girl must have some power over him.

"Nope. He may be one of the smartest guys I know, but I'd bet my last dollar that he'd deny it if asked. The dude is clueless at the moment."

I can't fault the guy for looking happy though. He deserves it, after everything he's been through.

DeShawn turns the conversation back to me before I can brace myself. "So, are you really going to look me in the eye and say you're not attracted to your tutor at all?"

No. Because I'd be lying.

Instead, I hedge. "I'm just helping a friend out, D."

When my phone vibrates in my pocket, I quickly pull it out and I'm shocked to see a message from Ari. She never texts at this hour, so hopefully something isn't wrong.

Ari: Congrats on the win! What a nail-biter!

Before I can tap out a thanks, a picture of her comes through with an avocado green mask plastered all over her face and a girl I don't recognize. Even with her face covered, her goofy expression is priceless and I can't help but grin at her antics. She is precious—even with that crap everywhere.

Ari: Sasha is totally on board for you helping me next weekend. She can't wait to meet you. Thanks again.

Me: Thank you and no thanks needed. Glad I can help. Looking forward to meeting her, too.

Ari: Gotta run. Cracking masks—time's up. See you Tuesday at our usual spot.

Shaking my head at the thought of peeling off a hard face mask, I quickly tap out my final response before returning my attention to DeShawn.

Me: The price of beauty. See you then.

When I look up, I find DeShawn's eyes dancing from me to my phone and his head shaking.

"What?"

"Oh, Z. You've got it just as bad as Drew. You're all dropping like flies, I tell ya."

"Whatever you say," I scoff.

"I know that look. Trust me, Zander, when I tell you— you'd better be very careful this weekend."

"You're delusional, DeShawn. Very, very delusional."

"I THINK I'VE GOT IT," I say, stretching onto my tiptoes from the last rung I'm willing to climb up this ladder. Sasha wants the tulle and twinkling lights to wrap the column from as high as possible. Since I'm a good head taller than everyone in the room, I've been deemed the master of all things high. But even with the ladder, it just isn't enough.

"Sash, I'm not sure how much higher I can go."

Instead of Sasha replying, I'm startled by a deep baritone I didn't know I'd been missing. "Need some help with that?"

Not wanting to draw attention to my reaction, I quickly offer stepping off the ladder. "If you want to hang out up here, you're more than welcome." Clearly, all of my five feet ten inches will only get me so far. In defeat, I admit, "I'm just not cutting it."

The moment my feet touch the floor, Zander surprises me again by leaning in and kissing me on the cheek in greeting. "Hey, beautiful. How was your morning?"

Talk about playing the doting boyfriend to perfection. He even has my heart racing and I know this is all for show. Pretending to be unaffected by his delicious musky scent, I casually reply, "It's been busy, but I'm glad you're here." Remembering my manners, I introduce Zander to the room, starting with Sasha. "Zander, this is my best friend and the soon-to-be bride, Sasha."

I almost lose it when Sasha catches Zander off guard by throwing her arms around him and pulling him in for a hug. "It's so nice to finally meet you. I've heard so much about you."

Zander briefly glances at me, then plays it off. "It's all good, I hope."

"Oh, only the best from my Ari." Then she quickly introduces him to the rest of the room, starting with her mom, then on to her cousin Jenna, aunt Ruth, and ends the introductions with her grandma. He takes the time to greet each then wins them all over with ease when he says, "If you don't mind me hanging out, I've got two free hands. Put me to work."

"Oh, you should be careful with those words." Sasha's grandma, Louanne, grins victoriously. "Now that we've got you, we may not let you go. But first, you'll have to fill us in on how you and our Ari met."

Thankfully Sasha comes to the rescue. "Oh, Grandma. Let's let them tell their story in their own time. We don't want to scare this nice man off *before* taking him up on his offer." Then she points to the column before us. "Do you think you can get these to the top?"

Grabbing the tulle from my hand, Zander chuckles.

"Alright. I see how it is." When he steps to the ladder, he pauses to look at Louanne. "And for the record, I met Ari outside the library on campus."

"That girl always did have her nose in a book," Gemma, Sasha's mom, muses and the room fills with laughter.

Yep. They've got me pegged.

Of course, with Zander's help, we hang the decorations with ease. But to my surprise, he doesn't stop with the columns. Nope, he moves tables and chairs and helps us decorate the entire room in nearly half the time we were expecting.

As soon as we finish the final item on Sasha's to-do list, she boldly announces to the room, "We have a few hours until we're meeting for the rehearsal dinner. Would you hate me if I ask you for one more favor?"

"What's that?" I ask, eyeing her suspiciously. I know without a doubt everything on her list is complete, so I can't wait to hear what she thinks she's forgotten.

"I'd meant to get some saltwater taffy for each of the tables tomorrow night. Could the two of you pick some up from my favorite store?"

Before I can turn to question her odd request, Zander answers for us. "Any flavors in particular?"

Rushing to her purse, her mother pulls out some cash and says, "Oh, that would be wonderful. It's the one thing I haven't gotten to since we arrived. I have everything for the party favors back at the condo we're renting, so just swing by when you're done and I'll make sure it's all bagged before tomorrow night."

"Oh, Gemma. I can do that," I offer quickly. She's got enough going on with all her family coming to town.

"I'm more than happy to help, too," Zander says without missing a beat as he reaches for my hand. "Is the candy shop within walking distance?"

Why does his large hand fit perfectly intertwined with mine?

As I stare into his beautiful brown eyes, it takes me a moment to remember he's asked a question. When his throat clears, I remember he's expecting an answer. "Uh, yeah. It's just a few blocks away."

"Well, then. We'll meet you at my parents' place," Sasha says with a wink as she grabs a hold of her mom and grandma's hands. "If we're lucky, we'll actually get some rest before the rehearsal dinner. We've been running ourselves ragged since breakfast this morning and I don't know about you, but I could use a break."

"Go. Relax." I assure them all. "Zander and I will take care of this."

Pulling me toward the exit, Zander gives the sexiest smile to the ladies in the room. "I'm sure you know Ari's number if you need anything else while we're out. Don't hesitate to call."

Instead of releasing my hand as I'd expect the moment we exit the banquet room, Zander links his fingers through mine, as if it's something we've done forever. Even as we enter the sidewalk and start walking toward the candy shop, he never lets go.

"How is everything with the wedding going so far? Have you had to deal with your ex much?"

I sigh in relief. "Thankfully I haven't run into him yet. He's not due in until this afternoon. He's picking up his grandma, Bernice, which is the least he can do since somehow, he's always been her favorite. He may have been a colossal asshole to me in the end, but he's always had a soft spot for Bernice."

"Where does she live?"

"She still lives on her own near Olympia, but with the weather being unpredictable this time of year, she'd rather not drive herself this far."

"So... if you don't mind me asking... how long did the two of you date?"

"Uh," I sigh, rubbing my nose, wondering where's the best place to start. He might as well know the quick and dirty version of our backstory. Then he can help navigate our weekend. "We were high school sweethearts. Though... I guess we started spending time together in middle school, so maybe that's not right. Anyway, he was a year older than me and ended up doing Running Start while we were in school, earning an Associate's degree in high school. Then he graduated with his business degree last spring and immediately started his career in Tacoma, while I've obviously stayed at CRU through the summer."

"Did... I mean... how..." Zander's never been one for a loss of words, so when he stammers over his thoughts, I quickly cut him off at the chase.

"Dylan didn't do well with distance. We barely lasted the summer before he gave me the *'It's not you, it's me'* speech."

"Holy shit. That's rich. How long did you all date?"

Shaking my head, I admit, "A little over four years... officially."

"Well... *officially*, Dylan's an idiot as he must have shit for brains to walk away from someone as smart and beautiful as you."

I'm not sure if it's the combination of Zander's expression or his bluntness. But, instead of the usual constricting tightness in my chest I've come to expect when I think about Dylan, I laugh. Like full-on belly laugh, and it's the release I never knew I needed.

"Thank you, Zander," I admit when my breathing returns to normal. And then I find myself replaying his words on a loop—wait, he thinks I'm beautiful?

I no sooner get the thought out when I hear my name being called from behind. "Ari? Is that you?"

My entire body tenses, as I'd know that voice anywhere. It's the same one that made many promises, yet broke every single one in an instant. Without missing a beat, Zander squeezes my hand as I slowly turn to face Dylan.

Just having Zander by my side gives me the confidence I'd momentarily lost. "Oh, hey, Dylan," as if this isn't the first time we've seen each other since we broke things off.

I'll admit, I'm relieved to find the girl he's supposedly dating nowhere in sight.

His face breaks into the smile that used to make me swoon, but oddly enough no longer has the potency. Before I can scrutinize his expression further, he interrupts my thoughts once again. "I thought that was you... but I wasn't sure." Then he shakes his head as he used to when he's gathering his thoughts. "Wow... you cut your hair. It looks great."

Okay. This is awkward. We haven't spoken in months and now we're talking about my hair?

"Uh, thanks."

Not letting go of me, Zander steps forward with an outstretched hand. "I'm Zander."

Dylan's eyes widen for a split second as if he's just noticed Zander's presence. But then his manners kick in and he forces himself to take Zander's outstretched hand. "Dylan."

Being best friends for nearly half my life, I can read Dylan like a book. So, when his eyes dart to mine, I clearly see confusion etched across his features before it quickly morphs into curiosity as he silently raises a brow as if he's asking, *who the hell is this guy?*

For a long moment, I stare back in challenge.

Like hell is it any of your business, Dylan. That ship sailed the moment you broke up with me.

As if he can hear the unspoken conversation between Dylan and me, Zander asks, "Are you a part of the wedding party?"

If I wasn't schooling my features, I'd likely laugh at Dylan's expression as his eyes roam between myself to Zander. Since Dylan and I are nearly the same height, he has to look up to meet Zander's gaze.

Clearing his throat, he answers, "Uh, yeah. I'm the brother of the groom and his best man.... And you are?"

Zander nods in understanding. "I'm Ariadne's boyfriend." Usually, I hate my name but the way it rolls off his lips sends shivers down my spine. Somehow, he makes my detested name sound sexy and I find my gaze sliding to Zander as he smiles with genuine pride. There's no malice to his words or egotism when he continues, "I'm here to help out where I can with the wedding and spend some much-needed time with her away from campus."

"Well… that's nice of you. I'm sure Colby and Sasha will appreciate that."

"Dylan. There you are. I've been looking for you everywhere," a high-pitched woman's voice announces. "I've got everything I need. We should get back to the hotel so I can get ready for dinner on time."

Instantly my attention is drawn to the curvy sandy blonde that strolls up beside Dylan and takes his hand. She only comes up to his shoulders and is the polar opposite of me. Not only is she short and curvy in all the right places, but her makeup is done to perfection. I'd bet my bottom dollar she's extremely high maintenance if her acrylic nails and false lashes are anything to go by. Don't get me wrong, under normal circumstances I'd say she's pretty if you're into that type of thing. Given the fact she's the one he cheated on me with, I just can't find it in myself to give her the chance she likely deserves.

He's the cheater—and that act alone reflects on him— not her.

But that doesn't mean I have to like her, either.

Before any of us can say anything or the situation gets even more awkward, Zander once again steps in and saves the day.

"We'd better get this errand run for Sasha before dinner, if you'll excuse us."

The blonde beside Dylan just stares at me as the color drains from her face.

Oh, she knows exactly who I am.

Not wanting to subject myself to another moment in Dylan and his girlfriend's presence, I nod at Dylan and let Zander pull me away.

Neither of us say anything as we walk to the store. The moment we are around the corner Zander stops and pulls me into the entry nook of a nearby shop. Leaning in, so that I'm completely blocked by anyone passing by, he whispers in my ear so only I can hear, "You okay?"

Am I okay? I don't even know how to feel, let alone what I feel. I knew we'd run into them—eventually. I just didn't expect it right here on the street.

At first, I look anywhere but at him, but when he patiently waits me out, I reluctantly meet his gaze and admit, "Seeing him took me off guard, I suppose."

"You're not in this alone, Ari. I've got you."

Zander's strong arms wrap around me, pulling me in for a hug, and between his tight hold, intoxicating scent, and steady heartbeat as I lay my head against his chest, I finally let myself relax.

"Just breathe, beautiful. I've got you."

I'm not sure how long we stand like this. It could be a minute or twenty. But his strength and certainty are more comforting than I'd ever expected.

Eventually, I pull back and meet his beautiful dark brown

eyes. "I'm good. Let's get that taffy and get back so we can relax a bit before dinner."

Zander peers behind his shoulder then turns to me and whispers, "Laugh."

What? Why the hell would I laugh?

"Trust me," he says as he brushes a strand of hair behind my ear and rests his palm against my cheek.

When he unexpectedly crosses his eyes and grins as a big puff of air blows all over my face, catching me by surprise, I giggle at his antics.

And then he takes my breath away as he leans in and plants an unexpected kiss on my lips.

"What the..." I mumble but then he pulls me closer. I'm caught off balance and gripping his shirt to stay upright. He kisses me once, twice, and again for a third time. When his tongue glides along the seam of my lips, I'm consumed by his taste and unexpectedly find myself kissing him back.

I'm not sure if it's his deliciously plump lips, the way he grips me as if he'll devour me whole, or the fact that I can no longer remember my name, let alone any troubles I may have had. And at this point, I don't even care. He tastes divine.

After all too short of a time, he breaks our kiss and pulls away, but I find I'm wanting more.

"What the hell was that?" I whisper in wonder and I'm not entirely certain if I'm speaking to him or myself in this moment.

With a triumphant grin, he smirks. "A kiss."

"I know what *that* was," I hiss out in irritation—again, I'm not sure who I'm directing my sudden annoyance at. This man could easily melt panties or hell—entire wardrobes away with kisses like that.

His grin turns cocky. "A damn fine kiss… if I do say so myself."

Glancing behind him, he grabs my hand. "I think the coast is clear. Dylan's at the end of the block. Let's go get that candy. And if you're lucky, I may just kiss you again before the night is through."

Oh my freaking god. Did he just say that?

Wait…. Is that a threat or a promise?

8

ZANDER

I HAVEN'T BEEN able to get that kiss out of my mind. I'm not sure what came over me. I saw Dylan in the distance and acted on impulse. There's no way I wanted that douche-canoe to see he may have rattled my strong and steady Ari. He doesn't even deserve to breathe the same air as her. She's a goddess and he's a prick as far as I'm concerned.

Mine? What the hell am I talking about?

Yes, she's *my* tutor—but that's it.

I may have taken the role as her fake boyfriend a little further than necessary as I stepped into that alcove. But all my reasons for kissing her vanished the moment my lips touched hers. All that mattered was taking her in and deepening our kiss the way I could've only dreamed of. In mere moments, she awakened something I've been holding back—And I'm not certain it's something that can be reburied.

Then she kissed me back and something shifted.

I have no idea what to make of it. All I know is it felt so

right holding her in my arms. Devouring her lips felt as natural as breathing.

On my drive out to the coast, I'll admit I had my doubts on whether or not we'd make our fake relationship believable. I mean, we barely know one another outside of a study room.

Yeah, those thoughts are long gone.

Not that I'd admit this to anyone—especially Ari—but I haven't had to act once throughout this entire afternoon. Being around her and her friends is not only fun, but something I could easily get used to. We play off each other with ease and gravitate toward one another like a couple who's been dating for years, rather than portraying a farce.

Sitting beside her at the rehearsal dinner, I find myself reaching for her hand under the table to rest it on my thigh. I've never been the touchy-feely sort of guy, but the way her hand feels in mine as we carry on casual conversations with the wedding party feels right. Thankfully, Dylan and his date —Tara, we later found out—are at the opposite end of the table. They're out of our direct line of sight and far beyond expected talking distance. This alone has Ari relaxing into me as we visit with Sasha and Colby's family.

"So... what are you studying in school?" Sasha's brother, Josh, asks as pie is served for dessert.

"Sports medicine with a minor in sports psychology." Eventually, I might go on to become a physical therapist, but I'll see where my game takes me first. I'm not stupid. I know there's only a four percent shot of me going pro, so I take school seriously. Like my mom always says, I won't count my chickens before they hatch. I've had my share of scouts watching me and with our championship last season, I know I'm at least on a few teams' radars. But I'd never mention this aloud as I won't jinx myself.

Josh is a few years younger than us, so I take no offense when he slowly looks me over from head to toe before asking, "Wait... are you an athlete?"

Ari laughs before I can respond.

"Is he an athlete? You do realize you're sitting across from one of the best ballers in the country, right?"

"I wouldn't go that far," I quickly interject, then look to Josh. "But sure, I can play."

"Okay, Mr. Modest. Where did you come from? You crush it on the court and I've never seen you shy about your skills."

How the hell do I respond without looking like a pompous ass?

Sheer adoration shines in Ari's expression and suddenly my chest tightens. Her expression in this moment mirrors my mom's when she attends a game. I know my worth on the court, but I'm not about to brag about it with practical strangers. Mom would have my ass. I may talk shit with the guys, but this isn't the place.

"Wait... you're *The Zander Williams* from CRU? I remember now. I watched you in the final four last season. Man, you're a beast on the court."

No matter how good I get, it's awkward as fuck to be described as an object, rather than a simple human being. I'll never be anything more than just Zander. Thankfully Ari must agree, too, because she rolls her eyes at Josh's enthusiasm. I swear I could kiss her for being on the same page.

"Thanks, man, we work great as a team," I quickly offer, hoping this conversation won't last long. This is a wedding after all and the focus should be on the bride and groom.

Thankfully Sasha's dad uses this moment to stand to tap his glass with his knife, gathering everyone's attention and my silent prayer is granted.

Clearing his throat, he stands. "I want to thank everyone for being here for this special occasion." Looking at his daughter, his eyes shine with unshed tears. "It seems like just yesterday you were standing on my toes as we danced across the living room. Now look at you... You're all grown up and it's Colby's turn to lead you around the dance floor."

"Aww... Daddy, I love you," Sasha interrupts.

Adoringly, he looks his daughter in the eye. "Love you, too, baby girl." Then he focuses his attention on Colby. "I couldn't have picked a better man for my daughter. I'm proud to gain another son." Awwws fill the room before her dad grins widely at his wife. "Now he can be the builder of bigger bookshelves and keep her gas tank off empty."

Ari shakes with laughter beside me and my attention zeros in on her. She is downright beautiful with her sheer abandon. Her eyes are glossy and I'm unsure if they'll fill with tears from laughing so much or the emotions of seeing her best friend get married.

Turning to me she fills me in on the joke. "It's true. I can't tell you how many times Sasha and I coasted into the station on fumes back in high school. I even bought her a gas can to put in the car for her birthday once, so we wouldn't get completely stranded."

"Please tell me you don't have that habit?" I tease.

Adamantly Ari shakes her head. "Nope. Not a chance. It only took actually running out of gas with her—once. No thank you. Besides my dad always says, *'it costs just as much to keep it on the top half as the bottom half of the tank.'* I never would have lived it down."

"The man's got a point."

"No kidding. I rarely let my tank go under a quarter, thanks to Sasha."

Placing an arm around her, I squeeze her shoulder. "Good to know we won't get stranded anytime soon."

Not that there will be a *we* beyond this wedding, but it wouldn't be the worst thing in the world to get stranded with Ari. I'm sure we could find something to occupy our time—especially those luscious lips and soft skin I can't stop touching.

Jesus, man, get it together.

It's not gonna happen.

As Sasha's dad says something else, I find myself watching Ari. Her skin's radiant and her minimal makeup makes her beautiful hazel eyes pop. Seeing her in her natural element brings a whole new light to her. She's not only fierce, but loyal, too. I can tell from just our afternoon's interaction she also loves deep and will do anything necessary to be here for her friend—including walking down the aisle with her ex, as they are the only members of the bridal party.

During rehearsal, I'm sure everyone could feel the tension when she was called up for duty. But leaning in I kissed her on the cheek and whispered, "You've got this. I'm right here if you need me." Somehow my words made her relax and her spine straighten taller.

Thankfully, she got through the entire rehearsal with ease —or at least she masked it well. By the way she pulled it off, you'd never know she'd been nervous about today.

I'm glad I could be here for her. She's an incredible person and she shouldn't have to go through hanging out with her ex and his new girl alone. I mean…. I know she would have her best friend, but Sasha's focus should be on her wedding, not Ari. I'm here, in her corner.

When Sasha's dad makes the room erupt in laughter again, I'm pulled back to reality.

The next thing I know, Dylan's standing beside her dad slapping him on the back and asking if he could say a few words. "As the best man, I have to say I'm so proud of my brother. It feels like just yesterday that Ari and I set you two up." Instantly, Ari stiffens in my arm and I'm on alert.

Dylan doesn't even spare Ari a glance and I feel her release the breath she'd been holding. "And look at you now—I guess little brothers do know a thing about what makes you happy."

Her best friend has her back when she laughs as she looks at Ari. "Well, Ari knew we'd be happy. She was relentless when it came to setting me up with Colby."

"And the rest they say is history." Colby goofily grins as he kisses his bride-to-be. "Because I couldn't imagine my life without you, Sasha."

Sighs from women can be heard from around the room, as Sasha radiates with love for him. I barely know them, but even a blind man could tell these two are it for each other. Just in their tone, adoration is evident.

Dylan clears his throat to break up their kiss. "Anyway... as I was saying.... Colby, you're not just my brother. You're one of my best friends. I truly wish both you and Sasha a lifetime of love, laughter, and happiness."

The room erupts with cheers and Dylan waits for the crowd to settle before finishing. "For the record, I've honestly never seen love look so good on either of you." Lifting his glass, he grins. "To the bride and groom-to-be, I love you both and I'm looking forward to finally having a little sister."

As everyone takes a sip from their glass, Ari turns to me. "I guess I'm up."

Standing where she is, Ari waits for the well wishes to end, then she raises her glass toward the couple of the night. "Sasha, I've known you since kindergarten. I knew the minute I saw that ratty ole' stuffed animal squeezed in your backpack, we'd be friends. We've been there for one another through thick and thin. Bad bangs and elegant ball gowns." This draws a chuckle from the crowd.

"I've watched you go through all your firsts. The good, the bad, the unmentionables..." She raises a brow at Sasha and the two of them share a laugh before she continues, "I've never been happier for you than when you found your forever love with Colby."

I'm surprised when she pointedly addresses Dylan.

"Yes, it's true. We went on their first date with them. However, I'm the one who plotted *shipping* them together. I always invited her along when I knew Colby was in town from college and it was *me* who got him to realize their four-year age gap wasn't a big deal."

"Thank God for that," Colby gushes. "I don't know where I'd be without your constant pushing."

Ari's smile beams as she waggles her brows. "I know… I was a pest—but I always meant well. But as you well know, I'm also often right." This makes the room fill with laughter again and Ari beams with pride.

God, her confidence is gorgeous.

"Just look at the two of you. You're perfect for one another—and no one can tell me any differently." Taking a deep breath, Ari slowly exhales. "But seriously. I love you both more than you'll ever know and I wish you the best of luck. I can't wait to see where this amazing adventure takes you."

Sasha's eyes gleam with unshed tears when she blows Ari a kiss and says, "Love you, too," as the room erupts with cheers as they drink from their glasses.

The moment Ari sits down, I lean in to whisper, so that only she can hear. "You did great. I'm proud of you."

"Thanks." She smiles as we watch the happy couple kiss once more.

When she sighs heavily, I can't tell if she's just tired or something is off. "What's wrong?"

"It's not a big deal."

Raising a brow, I call BS. "What is it, Ari? Just tell me. I know I'm just a guy, but when a girl sighs like that and says *it's not a big deal*, it's usually something. Sell it to someone else."

Her beautiful eyes roll, shaking her head in denial. With a

playful smirk, she whispers, "I'll tell you after dinner. I'd rather not talk about it now."

Okay, I can live with that.

Trying to change the subject, I ask, "What's next on the agenda?"

Shrugging she looks to Sasha. "We're just playing it by ear. We've already decorated the hall for tomorrow, and since the taffy's all sorted, I'm not sure what else needs to be done. Colby mentioned doing something on the beach, but I think that's just for the guys."

"Just let me know if you need help with anything," I offer. I can easily entertain myself, but I'd much rather help if I can —especially if it means spending more time with her.

It doesn't take long for Ari and me to immerse ourselves into the casual conversation around us. I'm relieved when I feel her body relax as I hold her hand once again. Eventually, people start saying they'll meet up with one another in the morning. Ari excuses herself for a moment to talk with Sasha privately.

I watch as they eagerly hug one another before talking animatedly. Each radiate happiness and their bodies shake with laughter from time to time. Eventually, Sasha leans in to hug her once more. As Ari walks away, Sasha says something else, but I don't catch it from our distance.

As Ari approaches she's shaking with a playful smirk. Instead of taking the chair beside me, she leans in and whispers, "You ready to get out of here?"

"Don't you have plans with Sasha?"

Laughing, she reaches for my hand and pulls me toward

the exit. "Oh, she'll be busy for the next hour or so. She and Colby are taking some time for themselves. They need a break from it all. They love their family, but as I pointed out—this wedding is about them—so they should do what makes *them* happy, not their parents."

"Fair point. But now that you've got an hour or so, wanna get changed into some warmer clothes and go for a walk?" She's wearing a beautiful black dress that wraps around her body and ties near her waist. It reveals the curves she's kept hidden under oversized sweatshirts at school and as much as I'd love to look at her all night, I want her comfortable in this cooler weather.

Walking to the elevators, she reaches for my hand. "Sure. Wanna meet me in the lobby when you're ready?"

Entering the elevator, I hit floor three for her and seven for me. "Just text me if you need more time."

9

ZANDER

NOT EVEN TWENTY MINUTES LATER, we're each dressed in CRU sweatshirts and sweats. If I didn't know better, you'd think we planned it. The only difference is she's wearing an open jacket over the top of her oversized sweatshirt.

When I spot Tara entering the lobby from the parking lot, I make a snap decision grabbing Ari's hand and walking toward the beach exit instead. "Now that we're alone, wanna tell me what was bothering you earlier?"

From the corner of my eye, I watch her lower lip roll under her teeth. In my short time of knowing her, I've learned this is her *thinking* face. "I'm not really sure where to start or if I can explain it effectively."

Giving her a light hip bump, I tease, "It's not like I'll judge you."

Once we're outside, I give her time to collect her thoughts.

It isn't until we get to the well-lit boardwalk that she opens up. "I'm not sure how to explain this, but seeing Dylan today, I realize I not only lost my boyfriend, but one of my best friends. Before we even thought of dating, we were truly friends. The only one ever closer to me than Dylan is Sasha."

"That makes sense. Losing any friend is difficult."

"Especially the way that I did. I keep thinking about how things were at the end. Things became routine and we both were complacent in our relationship. Truthfully, if we'd both been honest with one another, it had drifted back to more of a friendship than intimacy. We saw less and less of one another, but that still doesn't warrant his cheating."

"Nothing explains cheating. If you're ready to move on— end the relationship you're in. Period. It's not fair to anyone involved and you're just a selfish ass if you don't."

I can't even imagine her sense of betrayal—especially from someone you considered to be your closest friend. This takes his jackassery to a whole new level. He doesn't even deserve her thoughts.

"Exactly. If he had just been honest about his feelings, we would have never let things get so far gone—and we likely would have walked away as friends."

"Do people really walk away from dating someone for that long and remain friends?" I ask in disbelief. Reaching for her arm, I stop and stare down at her waiting for a response. "How the hell can that work?"

Sighing heavily, she looks to the sky then back to me. "I don't know. Before he cheated, we'd already stopped our intimacy due to distance. We'd just check in with one another daily and make plans every couple of weeks. Sometimes we wouldn't see one another for an entire month and honestly, I was okay with it."

"That still doesn't excuse his cheating."

"No, it doesn't. But I'm just so tired of hating him."

"So forgive him," I suggest. "Hate is extremely consuming."

"But…" she starts, but I interrupt so I can finish the rest of my thought.

Leaning in so that we're eye to eye and my message is clear, I finish. "Ari, forgiveness isn't for the offender, it's for yourself. If you let hate consume you, you'll never move forward with your life. Forgiveness is for you. So you can heal—not for the other person."

When her eyes drop to her hands, she says, "I guess I see your point."

Using a finger to lift her chin so her eyes will meet mine, I wait until I have her full attention. "Only you will know if that's the right choice for you, but you shine too bright to let him dim your light."

For a moment we just stare at one another. I have no clue what's spinning in that colossal brain of hers, but I hope she understands my message. He doesn't deserve her forgiveness, but I don't want her in pain by it either.

For years, I thought the opposite of love was hate. But as I've grown older, I realize I had it wrong. The opposite of love is indifference. Not that I'd know that from personal experience. No, I've had my mom and sisters to thank for that bit of wisdom. Each time my mom helped one of them through a heartbreak, she'd give the same speech I just gave Ari.

Nodding, Ari admits, "It was much easier to see him than I thought it would be. With Sasha marrying his brother, I'm sure this will be the first of many times we'll be around each other—so I'd better get used to it."

"True. The thing about forgiveness is you never have to say a word to him—to have peace in your heart."

Her eyes gleam with unshed tears and my heart nearly rips in half. "How did you get to be so wise?"

Reaching out, I brush a wayward strand of hair blowing in the wind behind her ear. "I've watched my sisters and friends go through breakups."

"So, this isn't from personal experience?"

"I've had my share of upsets, but I can't say I've loved anyone enough to be completely heartbroken."

"So... you've never been in love?"

Shrugging, I admit, "Never took the time to get close enough to someone. When I was younger, I dated a lot and had crushes, but eventually basketball took over my life. I'll date occasionally, but I can't say I've been in love."

"That's just..." she trails off and a flurry of emotions flit across her face.

Instead of letting her pity me, I admit another untold truth. "I'd never found someone worth laying my heart on the line for. It's not that I'm against love or going all in. I just never met the right one." Needing to get this subject off of me, I suggest, "You ready to keep walking?"

"Sure." Ari nods as we continue walking.

For the longest time, we walk in silence.

I'm stuck in my head wondering if I've made things better or worse by admitting my truth. I wish I knew what Ari was thinking, but at the same time, I need time so I can process the events of the day as well.

Ari is exactly the type of girl I'd let myself get attached to, if I had the time to date. With the season being underway, I barely have time to breathe, let alone devote to someone else. Ever since our championship game last season, I always wonder if a girl is with me for me—or for where I can get her.

Ari's genuine and true. She calls me on my shit and isn't afraid to tell me what she thinks. She truly has my best interests at heart when she's giving advice. She also sees through the hype of being a baller on campus and I've never had to put on airs with her.

It doesn't hurt that she's smart, sexy, and kisses like a vixen singing a siren call—each and every time we touch. Holy shit, if our kisses are that consuming, I can't even imagine what she's like between the sheets.

Nope—don't go there.

You're doing her a solid by being here for her this weekend.

Even if I pursued these feelings I'm developing, is she even in the right headspace? Clearly, she's still mourning her ex and I'd be nothing but a rebound to her. With the way my pulse accelerates when she enters the room, I can't afford to set myself up for failure like that. I've got too much at stake with the season underway and scouts looking at me for next year.

Before I know it, we reach the end of the boardwalk, turn

around, and walk back toward our hotel. I'm not even sure how we've made it this far, but seeing the tall buildings near the turnaround at the ocean are now small in the distance, I quickly realize I must've been stuck in my head longer than I thought.

We walk for a while longer in comfortable silence. Eventually I realize I need out of my own headspace, so I switch my focus. "What's going on in that head of yours?"

"Just taking in what you've said."

"I didn't mean to upset you."

"You didn't. If anything, you've helped—once again." Peeking at me from the corner of her eye, her face lights up with a smile.

"Glad I can help. It's what I'm here for."

"I seriously don't know what I'd have done without you. I'd been dreading seeing Dylan again and having your support means everything."

"No need to thank me. I've had a great time so far—and it got me away from campus. It's a win for us both."

"If you say so," she draws out. When her beautiful laugh fills the air, I know all is good with her.

"I do—so shush. I'm not gonna listen to you talk shit about yourself. You may as well accept my word as truth."

Rolling her eyes, she chuckles again. "Oh, Zander, what am I gonna do with you?"

Knowing her question is rhetorical, I let it go.

"What are you doing tomorrow morning? I feel bad leaving you alone while I get ready for the wedding."

Since the wedding isn't until four, she and Sasha have

plans at the salon and spa here in the hotel. Then there are pictures and God only knows what else that goes into the details of a wedding.

"Don't you worry about me. I've got a king-sized bed with my name on it and I don't have to check out until noon."

Arching a brow, she asks, "You're really gonna sleep all day?"

"Heck no, but I'm gonna at least sleep past eight. Then I'll probably work out and get some homework done."

"Since I'm staying another night, why don't I give you a key to my room. You can hang in there until the wedding. Sasha and I will be gone by nine and we're getting ready in a room near the ceremony."

"You sure it won't be a bother?"

I'd been wondering how I'll fill the four hours between check-out and the wedding. If I could knock out my homework for the week, I'd be ahead when we go on the road for back-to-back games.

"Not at all. Other than sleeping, we'll barely be there. Someone may as well get some use of it. Besides—then you won't be dressed up for hours with no place to go."

She has a point. I have no trouble wearing a suit as I'm required to wear them weekly, but Seaside's a casual town and I'd stick out like a sore thumb wandering around.

"Okay, if you insist."

Unexpectedly, Ari does a little hop as she claps her hands together as if that's the best thing she's heard all year. "Great. I'll stop by the front desk to get a spare key so we won't have to worry about meeting tomorrow."

I love that something so small could make her happy.

She has no idea the lengths I'd go to keep that smile on her face.

And that's how I end up with her key burning a hole in my pocket as I walk alone to my room.

10

———————

ZANDER

I TOSSED and turned last night regretting our goodbye. We had that stereotypical goodbye at the elevator. It would've been so easy to bend down and kiss her. I wanted to—trust me. But I also didn't want to cross a line I wasn't sure I could return from.

Besides, there was no one around to perform our charade for and I wasn't prepared for her to call me on it. So, after staring at her for a long moment, I simply said goodbye as I exited the elevator.

Nothing about my feelings for Ari are a farce though—but I can barely admit it to myself, let alone her.

"We've made a deal," I remind myself as I force myself to run along the shore. "I'm only here as her pretend boyfriend."

Yes. I've resorted to talking to myself.

Thankfully I'm alone on the beach and even if I were close, the breeze would make my words lost in the wind.

This is how I process.

That and exercise. The gym at the hotel wasn't worth spending my time in, so I opted for a run instead.

I've been running for only fifteen minutes and I think I've gone in the wrong direction because I'm running toward the cove on the south end of the beach. I'd thought for sure there would still be some beach to run along, but I'm quickly finding out it's nothing but a rock wall. I have plenty of time until I have to check out, so I slow my pace and jog to one of the rocks closer to where surfers are heading out into the water.

I've only been in the Pacific Ocean a handful of times since arriving in Washington. I learned the hard way it rarely gets above sixty—even in the summer. So, I'm not surprised that everyone's wearing either wet or dry suits as they paddle out to catch a wave.

I shiver at my first memory of the Pacific Ocean. Drew took me and his roommates DeShawn and Grey to see it for the first time sophomore year. We were all stoked and couldn't wait to dive in. He laughed his ass off when the three of us went barreling into the water on a seventy-degree day. The moment we plunged through the incoming waves and completely submerged ourselves, there was instant regret. It was worse than a polar-bear plunge. The water was freezing and I couldn't get out fast enough. The worst part is, he got video of our entire escapades and showed the entire team what idiots we were. We didn't live that down for a long time—well, until the next prank was pulled.

It's something we do as a team—pull pranks. For some reason, it's how we've bonded off the court—though it's all done in fun. No one ever expected this particular one from him. Drew's the most straitlaced of us all—and I think that's what made it so good though, if I'm being honest. I'm sure he'll be getting acceptance letters for med school any day now—or at least I hope so.

Just thinking about Drew brings me back to my conversation with DeShawn on the bus.

Would it be so bad if I were to see what happens between Ari and myself?

Somehow Drew's pulled his stubborn head out of his ass and is giving it a go with his lab partner. I wonder if Ari and I have something real? Or are these feelings due to forced proximity?

Don't get me wrong, I've always thought she was gorgeous. But as I've gotten to know her over these past few weeks, I know that my attraction goes beyond the physical. I've just never let myself think beyond our working relationship. There's no doubt losing her as a tutor would impact me. The bigger question is—how will I feel if I don't take a chance with her?

Memories of working with my grandfather in the yard during the summer while my mom was at work flood my mind as I stare at the waves crashing over and over against the sandy shore. Whenever I had a difficult decision to make he'd always say, "You know, Z, when you get to be my age, you'll suddenly find you regret the chances you didn't take, rather than the ones you tried and they didn't turn out the way you'd expect. Don't be afraid to dream big, take that risk and follow your heart. Even if things don't turn out the way you'd expect— you've gotta ask yourself, what if it turns out even better?"

Suddenly, as if I've been hit over the head, an epiphany strikes.

Jumping up from the rock, I sprint down the beach back to the hotel. As I run, I know one thing is certain. I may not have everything worked out, but I'm one step closer than I was. I finally have a plan in this thick head of mine.

WANTING to stay out of the way, I remain in Ari's room until nearly three-thirty. I've been ready for a while and I just can't sit in this room any longer. As I walk through the lobby, I see others dressed up walking into the banquet room where the ceremony will be held. Once inside the room I take a seat near the aisle we created last night during set-up, so I can get a view of Ari as she walks down it.

As the room fills, I scroll through my favorite social media apps. For the first time since we met, curiosity gets the better of me and I land on Ari's profile. A smile pulls at my lips when I find her profile pic is from last night.

Damn. She's gorgeous.

That wrap dress fits her like it was made for her.

When I click on her photos, I'm surprised to find more photos from last night already uploaded. Well—she's been tagged in them because the rest of her account is set to private and that's all I can see. But that doesn't stop me from looking. My heart stops when I get to one of the two of us tagged by Josh.

The caption reads *#couplegoals*.

Holy shit. Not only is it a fantastic image, but in this candid shot, I'm leaning into her and our foreheads practically touch. We're both smiling as if we're madly in love and we're so lost in one another the room disappeared.

Ari's absolutely breathtaking and I don't look so bad myself.

Without a second thought, I tap on the photo, saving it to my phone. No matter what comes between us, I want to remember that moment forever. I've truly enjoyed my time with her this weekend and seeing her happy has made this trip worth it.

When the noise in the room settles, I glance up and realize the ceremony is starting. Dylan and Colby have escorted the mothers down the aisle and are taking their place next to the minister in front of the decorated arch.

How long was I lost in looking at Ari?

When the processional music starts, I pivot to the door I know Ari's waiting behind. The moment it opens, my breath hitches in my throat and my mouth dries instantly. Ari's standing there waiting for her cue with a beautiful smile and stunning dress. The entire room could go up in flames and I doubt I'd notice anything but Ari.

Her hair's in some fancy up-do that accentuates her beautiful cheekbones and makes her eyes pop. She's wearing more makeup than usual, but it only brings out her natural beauty. As my eyes roam down her body, I swear my heart almost rockets out of my chest. Words can't even describe how Ari looks. It is beyond perfection.

The deep red dress is sleeveless with columns of gathered

fabric coming over each of her shoulders flowing over her ample breasts and at the same time wrapping her waist perfectly. The dress itself is modest yet completely sensual at the same time. I'm not sure where the material goes once it hits her waist, but it flows almost whimsically into what my sisters called an A-line down to the floor.

The moment she takes a step forward, a sexy muscular leg slips through the slit of the dress and I nearly swallow my tongue. Ari's been holding out on me. As an elite athlete, I know how much time it takes to make muscles that tone. She obviously has never skipped arm or leg day. How have I not noticed her before?

Compared to the frumpy sweatshirts she wears on campus, clearly, I shouldn't have judged a book by its cover. Ari's definitely been keeping a few chapters to herself, as she's absolutely stunning. Wanting to capture the moment, I pull out my phone and grab a shot or maybe ten as she walks down the aisle.

This dress is the perfect combination of elegant, yet subtly sexy. Though what makes it sexy is Ari herself. Her beauty shines as her confidence soars as she approaches me. As she passes, I finally get why others are gasping in awe and adoration. There's an elaborate almost corset like back with straps of fabric crisscrossing her entire back, making my entire body stand up, taking notice. My eyes roam from her shoulders to her round ass taking in the intricate pattern.

Holy hell, Ari is hot.

The moment Ari takes her place, I'm forced to take my eyes off her because the music introducing the bride begins.

Standing, I note Sasha's beauty in a dress similar, yet more extravagant as it's white and filled with lace and clearly meant to be the focus of the day. She's a beautiful bride yet the moment she passes, my attention immediately turns to the gorgeous maid of honor next to her.

No matter how hard I try to focus on the bride and groom during the ceremony, my eyes remain on Ari. I'm aware of a poem being read, vows being said, and prayers made. By the time the groom kisses his bride, I couldn't tell you one specific detail about the happy couple. But I could tell you how often Ari shifted her weight, the way her eyes filled with tears in happiness for her friend, and how she visibly stiffened as she took Dylan's hand to walk down the aisle. I doubt anyone would notice, but I did and it bothered me.

As everyone exits to greet the happy couple in the hall, I help the remaining friends and family convert the room for their reception. By the time the bridal party returns, we're ready for them.

As people drift in, they find a table and get themselves drinks from the bar. Since I don't drink during the season, I grab myself a Coke and choose a seat near Josh when he motions to me from across the room. Thankfully, Sasha didn't assign seats or force Ari next to Dylan all night, so I save a seat for her at the table as well.

I feel the moment she walks into the room when the hair on my neck tingles. My eyes gravitate to her as she strides across the wooden floor. Standing, I meet her in the middle. Needing to touch her, I pull her in and quickly kiss her on the cheek. "You. Look. Incredible."

"Thank you." A light laugh escapes and her eyes twinkle as she looks me up and down. "You don't look so bad yourself."

"Should we put that bouquet at our table? I've saved you a seat."

Looking to the bar, she sighs, "I could use some water."

Pointing in Josh's direction to know where our seats are, I suggest, "Go sit beside him and I'll grab your water. Want anything else?"

"Water's fine for now. I'll grab a glass of wine with dinner."

The line will only get longer so I ask, "White or red?"

"White, please and thank you," she says, leaning in to kiss my cheek. In her heels, she's only a few inches shorter than me and I love being with a woman where my height difference isn't problematic.

By the time I've returned, she's deep in conversation with others at the table. I slide into the seat beside her, after handing her the water she'd asked for. When she pats my leg as a thank you, my hand covers hers and she flips her palm to link her fingers with mine.

How can being with Ari be this easy?

I know this is supposed to be an act, but nothing about this feels fake. Not allowing myself to get lost in my head, I just enjoy this moment with Ari and her friends. If all I get is this time with her, I'm not wasting it.

We carry on conversations with the rest of Sasha's family and before I know it, dinner is served and toasts are made. Then it's time for the couple's first dance and the father-daughter dance.

I love how emotional Ari gets watching her best friend's

happiness. Mom always said you should pick your friends by how they judge others' success. I've never seen anyone more genuine than Ari. And she proves it when she's forced to dance with Dylan.

I watch, ready to step in as Ari's posture stiffens. After a few words are said, she relaxes slightly. Maybe our conversation about forgiveness helped because eventually, she even laughs at something he says. The moment the DJ asks the audience to join in the dancing, her eyes dart to mine and I'm on my feet, closing the distance between us.

"May I cut in?" I ask once I'm standing beside them.

MY JAW DROPS when Dylan smiles and taps Zander on the shoulder. "Sure thing, man. Take care of this one. She's special."

"I have every intention." Zander nods in agreement.

"No matter what happened between us, I wish her the best. She deserves it."

"I couldn't agree more," Zander says, taking my hand.

What reality did I just step into?

Sure, he apologized earlier today for the way things ended, and the tension between us eased, but I never expected him to share those thoughts with Zander.

The minute Dylan steps away, Zander pulls me close and starts to dance. I expected the traditional high school sway, not to be completely swept off my feet.

"Uh, how did you learn to dance so well?"

Smirking, he twirls me once and shrugs. "I have a mom

and sisters who love dancing. Mom made me take lessons for more agility on the court. It comes in useful from time to time."

When the song switches to something faster, he changes tempo with ease and I release all the tension I've felt from the day with a laugh. "Very useful. What other tricks do you have up your sleeve, Zander Williams?"

Pulling me close, I feel his chest rumble with laughter as his eyes waggle. "Now why would I tell you that? How else am I supposed to keep you coming back for more?"

"Oh, so that's how we're playing this?"

Shrugging with feign innocence, he pulls my body through an intricate move, making me feel like I might be a pretzel. But he simply spins me out only to pull me close again, resting his hand on my hip and stares into my eyes as we move along with the beat. "The only games I play are on the court, Ari."

My belly flips and my entire body tingles in anticipation of a kiss with the heated look he's giving me.

Ohmigod, did I just swoon?

Before I can process my thoughts, his lips slant over me and he presses them to mine.

It's quick. It's punishing. And when he pulls back to spin me once again, it's making me want more. For now, I'll settle being in his arms as we dance around the room, but I need those lips on mine again soon.

I'm pulled away for some pictures and to help Sasha in holding her dress while she uses the restroom. If this doesn't prove my loyalty as a friend, I'm not sure what will.

As she washes her hands at the sink, she stops and turns to me with a goofy grin. "You like him."

"Colby? Of course, I do."

Swatting at my arm she says, "No, Ari. I'm talking about Zander."

"Sash, you know it's all an act, remember?" I pointedly remind her.

"Cut the crap, Ari. This is me and I know you. Hell, I've never even seen you look at Dylan the way you're looking at him."

"You have your honeymoon goggles on—and just want everyone around you to fall in love."

Squealing with excitement, she rushes in for a hug. "Of course, I do. But seriously, that man likes you just as much. He hasn't taken his eyes off you all afternoon."

"You're supposed to focus on your happiness today, not mine."

"So... he makes you happy?" Her voice rises three octaves in pure excitement and it's then I recognize my mistake.

I roll my eyes to play it off. "Not the point. He's only here as a favor."

"I wish you'd open your eyes and unlock the gates to that organ you so often ignore. Stop being rational and just feel."

"I feel..." I hedge and even I can hear the defensiveness in my tone.

"I know. But remember it's okay to take risks. I'd hate for you to miss out on something wonderful because you're too stubborn to see what is standing right in front of you."

When I just stare at her in disbelief, she points over her shoulder.

"You know... he's right out there, about yay big," she holds her hand high in the air, "and is the epitome of tall, dark, and handsome. You're lucky I met Colby first, or you'd have some competition... oh, get that look off your face. I'd never make a move on your man—even if Colby wasn't in the picture. Besides, I'd bet my last buck Zander only has eyes for you."

So much to unpack from that statement. "Uh... he's not my man."

Raising a brow in challenge she crosses her arms over her chest. "He could be..."

When the distinct beats of "The Wobble" waft through the door, she grabs my hand and says, "Just think about it. Now come on—let's dance before I miss my favorite song."

The moment we reach the dance floor, what I see stops me in my tracks.

There's Zander front and center, teaching Sasha's grandma the moves so she can dance with everyone else. His jacket's been tossed on his chair and he fills out his black button-up shirt perfectly. As he turns away from me with the crowd and wobbles his perfectly sculpted ass to the beat, it's all I can do to keep my jaw from dropping on the floor.

"Come on!" Sasha hollers, taking a place near the front to dance with her grandma.

As I make it to the floor, the crowd pivots and Zander's eyes meet mine. Forget about melting, that look alone could make my panties disintegrate on command. He is sexy as hell and seeing his big heart as he points out what to do next for Louanne makes my heart swell.

Yes, Sasha's right. I'm falling for him.

I just don't know what to do about it.

Instead of getting lost in my head, I join him and get lost in the music.

The song switches to a slow one, Zander reaches for my hand and I willingly take it. Pulling me close he whispers so only I can hear, "You smell amazing."

I feel his lips brush under my ear and leave a tender kiss.

"Hmmm... I could get used to that," escapes my lips without permission.

I feel him squeeze me tighter as "I've got more where that comes from" sends shivers down my spine. But before I can get carried away in this feeling, he straightens to his full height and spins me out for a twirl.

The heat in his eyes makes the sudden shiver in my spine roll to my extremities. I know without a doubt—he's no longer playing a part. No one can be this convincing.

But what does this mean for our arrangement after the weekend ends?

ZANDER

HAVING Ari in my arms on the dance floor makes the evening pass by in a blink. I just can't get enough of her. I love the way she shivers when I kiss the column of her neck, as well as the way she lets me lead her around the dance floor all night.

Of course, as the evening goes on, she tends to her maid of honor duties and dances with her best friend as well. But I love that she includes me in all that she can.

After the crowd says goodbye to the bride and groom, many of the guests begin dispersing as well. Now all that's left is the couple's core friends who've agreed to clean up. I make quick work of stacking chairs with Josh and moving tables to the storage area, while others divvy up the rest of the to-do lists.

Before I know it, everything's been taken care of and I'm walking Ari back to her room. After making sure she's settled, I'll grab my things and get on the road so I can meet my trainer in the morning. It's still early enough that I'll easily make it back to campus before midnight.

The moment we step into the elevator, Ari closes the distance between us and reaches for my tie pulling me closer. "There's been something I've been dying to do."

"Really? What's that?" I play along with her sudden change in demeanor.

Reaching a hand behind my neck, she pulls so that I'm a mere breath away from her lips. "This," she whispers as she brings my lips to hers.

We'd been flirting all night and from the sexy gleam in her eyes, we might have been playing with matches as well. Because the moment her lips touch mine, an inferno builds inside of me and I kiss her back for all I'm worth.

I need this woman more than I need my next breath. I've been holding back while we were in public, but now that we're finally alone, I can show her how I really feel. When her manicured nails scrape the short hairs at my scalp as she pulls her body closer against mine, she feels incredible. Through the thin fabric of our clothes, her heat consumes me and I need more.

When the elevator dings, we break apart, panting.

Apparently, we neglected to actually press the button to move the freaking elevator. In a split decision, I lean against the wall pulling her in front of me to hide my raging boner. There's no way I want Sasha's grandma or anyone seeing just how little room is left in my trousers. Of course, we couldn't be lucky enough to have some random stranger join us.

Nope—as the doors slide open, Dylan and his dad step into the elevator.

Talk about a boner killer.

He and his dad both nod in greeting, but it's his dad who speaks up. "It's good to see you again, Ari." Then he glances at me before returning his attention to her. "You've been like a daughter to me for years. No matter what went on with you and Dylan, I want you to know I'm so proud of the woman you've become. I'm glad to see you happy and healthy."

When the elevator stops on his floor, he steps toward the door and says, "Don't be a stranger, ya hear. I still love ya, kid." Then he turns to me. "Zander, it was nice meeting you. Thanks again for all your help tonight." With a tip of his head, he holds the door from closing, "See you at brunch tomorrow?"

"I'll be there," Ari says, then quickly adds, "But Zander has a meeting with his trainer back at campus."

"Ah... that's right. Best of luck to your season. Keep killin' it on the court."

"Thank you, sir."

And now we're left riding up to our floor with Dylan.

This isn't awkward or anything.

And I must've done something to piss off the gods, because... of course, he's on the same floor as Ari.

Thankfully it's only three floors and the ride's short, but no one in this shrinking elevator is comfortable.

When the doors slide open, Dylan steps out and turns to Ari as we exit. Reaching out his hand to me he says, "It was great to meet you. Good luck with your season."

Shaking his hand, I leave it at, "Thanks."

I'm sure as hell not saying meeting him has been a pleasure. But then again, if he hadn't been an assclown, I wouldn't have had this time with Ari.

Ari's heavy sigh says it all after he disappears around the corner in the complete opposite direction of her room.

Rolling her eyes, she reaches for my hand and walks the three doors down to her room.

"Sorry about that," she mutters.

"Don't. You have nothing to be sorry about."

Reaching for my wallet, I pull out her key and hand it to her. "Might as well return this."

"Thanks." She swipes the door open and steps through, pulling me with her.

The minute the door shuts, she turns and steps closer to me. Reaching for my tie like she'd done in the elevator, the mood of the room shifts.

"Now... where were we?" She grins, pulling me closer.

She kisses me with even more intensity than before. When our kiss breaks, it's hot as hell when Ari backs me up against the door. Running a finger from my temple to my chin, she holds my gaze. "For the record, I've been fantasizing about this since our first dance tonight."

"I'll never forget to push the elevator button again," I promise, then sober because I need to know we're on the same page. "But am I the one you want kissing you right now?"

As much as I don't want to know the answer, I ask because that conversation in the elevator may have rattled her, and emotions may be running high.

"I'm positive." Leaning in, she brushes her lips against

mine. "You're a phenomenal kisser and I'm not done with you yet."

My deep laughter fills the room. "Is that right? Well, don't let me stop you."

Gripping my shirt, she pulls me close and kisses me so completely, I nearly forget my name. It's hot as fuck and my hands roam along the intricate straps along her back, up to her hairline and down to grip her ass through the plethora of fabric in her skirt.

Sweet Baby Jesus, how thick is this skirt?

Before I can contemplate it further, her leg slips out through the slit and slides against my thigh.

Oh. My. Hell.

Her heat radiates along my pants and I need to feel more.

Eventually she breaks the kiss and pants, "Can we... get rid of this tie—for now?"

In a well-practiced move, I reach up to loosen the tie like I've done countless times for games. "That good?"

Ari's playful nod makes my dick twitch in my pants. "So much better." Reaching up, she unbuttons the top two on my shirt. "Now this." She kisses down the column of my neck. "I could get used to."

All I can do is lean my head against the door and enjoy the sensations she sets off inside me. With each button she unfastens, she kisses my neck lower.

She feels... fucking incredible with her body against mine.

I let her have her way for as long as I can manage.

But before I completely lose my shit in the best way possible, I take control of the situation.

Reaching for her chin, I bring her swollen lips to mine. "I need your lips, Ariadne." Slanting my lips over hers, I devour her. When our tongues join in the mix and our bodies move along one another, I can't get enough. I need more.

Without breaking our kiss, I grip her ass and turn us to explore her body as she relaxes against the door.

Her hands roam my neck and into my hair as I kiss along her jaw and across her collarbone. Her moans let me know I'm on the right track by the way her breath hitches.

She's a fucking goddess and I've never felt luckier than I am in this moment. After all, she wants me... and all my worries from this morning were for nothing.

As her exposed leg wraps around mine, my fingers do what they've been dying to all night. Slowly, I drag the tips of my fingers from her calf, up and along her knee, and up her thigh.

"Oh, Zander. That feels amazing," she pants, arching her body into mine. "I love your skin on mine."

"Me, too, beautiful," I whisper. When my hand reaches the panty line at her ass, I lean in and kiss her for all I'm worth. It's sexy as hell as her heel scrapes along the back of my thigh as her body moves in tune with mine.

When I feel a tugging sensation at the back of my shirt I break our kiss long enough to pull both my button up and undershirt over my head and throw it on the floor.

Ari's eyes widen as she gasps before her delicate fingers trail over the tattoo along my pecs and along my torso.

"See something you like?"

"Don't take this the wrong way, but you're absolutely beautiful. I knew you had tattoos, but now that I get to see them up close and personal, I need to run my tongue along every square inch of them."

"Only if you let me do the same." I challenge.

"But... I don't have any tattoos," she says, confused.

Leaning in, I pull at the fabric covering her perfect cleavage and run my tongue along the beautiful swell. "I'll need to lick every square inch of you to make sure."

Using the slit of her dress to my advantage, my hand runs along her thigh to grip her ass. After giving it a sensual squeeze, which I'm rewarded with a deeper arch of her back and moan from her luscious lips. Oh my hell.

As if they have a mind of their own, my fingers slide around the front of her panties and cup her mound. Her breath hitches and nails scrape against my back, and her mouth devours mine. As I play along the edge of her panties, Ari begs between kisses, "Zander..."

"Tell me what you need, Ari. I'll give it to you," I demand, sliding my fingers along the fabric once more.

"Stop teasing me already..." The moment I slide my fingers under the silky cloth and trace them along her seam, she makes the most guttural noise. My dick hardens instantly to granite. "Right there. Please... touch me right there."

Now that she's given me the go-ahead, I eagerly slide my middle finger from her core to her clit until it's slick with all that is her. While I'm getting her ready, I sensually suck on that spot that drove her crazy on the dance floor—and she doesn't disappoint.

She's so fucking responsive.

Her fingers dig into my back and she arches giving me

more access to her beautiful body. With my free hand, I push at the fabric covering her breast. But it barely moves.

"Tape. There's... uh... right there... don't stop.... Tape keeping... this dress in place. It's everywhere. Ohmigod, Zander, I just want to feel you everywhere."

As my finger keeps a steady rhythm sliding in and out of her dripping pussy, I circle her clit with my thumb. She writhes against the door and she tightens her leg around my thigh. As much as I'd love to play with her nipples with my tongue, I don't want to hurt her by ripping off the tape. Giving up on devouring her breasts for the time being, I drag my tongue along the spot that drives her wild at her neck and I'm instantly rewarded when she quivers uncontrollably.

Her body tightens as my name is repeated over and over. I can feel she's almost ready to spiral out of control, but she's not quite there. I'm not sure if it's the come-hither motion I press against her front wall, the sucking on her neck, or the squeezing of her breast as I massage it through the silky material that makes her suddenly stiffen like a board. When her inner walls pulse heavily and my hand soaks with her pleasure, I know she's coming—hard. And it's the most beautiful thing I've ever seen. She pulls my body as close as humanly possible and I nestle my head into her neck to ride out this wave with her.

When her body stops quaking, our ragged breaths regulating are the only sounds in the room. Eventually, her body relaxes and her leg slides over my ass to the floor. Knowing she's still in fuck-me heels, I wait until she's steady to pull my fingers from her warmth.

If she's this responsive with only my hand, I can't wait to see what she'll do when I taste her.

"You okay?" I ask, bringing my hand to my lips.

She nods silently, but her eyes widen as I suck the juices off my finger and inhale deeply. "You taste fucking incredible, Ari. If getting you off was a full-time job, we'd never leave the bedroom."

"That is…" She watches me inhale heavily again trying to make her scent linger in my brain. "Fucking hot. Please tell me you brought some condoms because after watching you do that, I'm already dripping with need for you again."

Leaning in, I kiss her until we both break away gasping from lack of air.

"Wait…" She gasps. "What time is your appointment tomorrow?"

"Nine," I say, puzzled. Why the hell is she thinking about that now?

"It's only a two-hour drive—do you think if you left by six you'd make it there on time?"

"Oh, hell yes. Who the hell needs sleep if it means I'm spending the night with you."

Grinning from ear to ear, she nods, then cocks her head to the side with a puzzled expression "You never said… do you have condoms? Or do we need to pray there's a convenient store open at this hour?"

How do I answer that without looking like a total player?

Rubbing my nose, I'm embarrassed to say, "I uh… always keep a box in my travel bag because you never know when someone will need some. But I uh… haven't used any for myself in..." I look to the ceiling as I do the math. "Uh... since the end of summer. I get tested regularly—and I'm clean. But to answer the question you asked... yes, I do have condoms."

"God, you're adorable." She leans in and kisses me chastely. "I haven't had sex since last spring and after Dylan I got tested. I'm clean, too. I'm dying to have you inside me. If you can ring out an "O" from me in record time with only your finger, I'm dying to find out what the rest of you can do."

"Okay, how the heck do we get you out of this contraption you call a dress?"

LOOKING DOWN AT MY DRESS, I start tugging and the tape hurts like a bitch to pull off. Don't even get me started on unwrapping the corset in the back or the thousands of bobby pins in my hair. If I knew Sasha wouldn't give me shit about it, I'm tempted to cut myself out of this thing so I can be naked with Zander.

"Um... that's a great question."

"Turn around, maybe I can help?"

I turn around to face the door. I have tape along the entire bottom edge of the dress at my lower back, to keep my ass where it's supposed to be. I hear the zipper slide down, but other than revealing the red lacy panties I'm wearing, it does nothing in terms of removing the dress.

"Those are sexy as fuck," he says as he kisses through the strappy corset. "So is this dress. I'd hate to do anything to ruin it."

"Ugggg... I love this dress. I feel amazing in it, but I'm

seriously tempted to rip it to shreds to get out of it. I don't want to wait any longer to be with you."

"God, I love it when you're needy. What do you want me to do?"

"As much as I'd like our first time to be in a bed, what do you think about getting creative and living out the rest of the fantasy you just created in my mind?"

"Okay, I'm intrigued. Tell me more," he says as he kisses that spot along my neck I love so much.

"Mmmmm.... I like that..." I moan.

"Ari... tell me about this fantasy."

"You taking me against the door just now was hot as hell. I've only read about things like this in books and experiencing it in real life is... just... beyond words."

When his entire body presses into mine from the back I feel his sexy pecs through the cutouts of my dress and the way his breath tickles my neck makes me dripping with need.

The next thing I know, his warmth is gone and he's gathering the material in his hands. "Let's put this slit to good use," he suggests.

"What do you mean?"

Pulling the fabric from the slit in the front, he gathers the skirt and it slides up my body. When my ass is entirely exposed to the cool air of the room he says, "Press your hands against the door."

Holy hell, his command alone soaks my panties.

Leaning in, he kisses the base of my neck where it meets my shoulder. Then he drapes the excess material over my right arm, so that it's entirely out of the way.

His voice is husky as he tells me exactly what he wants. "I'm gonna slide your undies off, but let's keep those sexy heels on."

The thought of what he's envisioning makes my core clench hard. He's like a dream come true. My throat is dry when I whisper, "This is so much better than my fantasy."

"I promise. We'll take all the time in the world to get you out of this properly. I definitely want you in this dress again. But I am hard as a rock seeing you in this sexy as fuck get-up."

Gripping my hip, the warmth from his large hand nearly has me combusting on the spot.

At the same time, his other hand slides around my waist then down across my mound.

When I can't take it anymore, I beg, "Please... Zander. Take them off and get inside of me. I wanna feel you."

Looping his thumbs into my panties at the waist, he slowly slides them down. I feel his warm breath at my ass, right before he leans in to kiss my cheek softly. As my underwear slides down he groans loudly and gives my ass a nip.

Holy shit... he bit my ass... "That was hot."

As if he has all the time in the world, he carefully lifts one leg, then the other to remove my panties completely.

"Keep your hands on the door and step back so you're leaning forward," he says, guiding my hips right where he wants me.

As his hand caresses my ass, he gently spreads my legs further apart.

His gruff voice fills the room. "Does this fantasy of yours have my pants on or off?"

"You were in too much of a hurry," I pant, arching into him further.

"On it is then," he says as his fingers trail around my upper thigh to my dripping wet sex.

Slowly his fingers slide into me while his other hand presses on my lower back, bending me further forward. "Right there," he says as the heat from his body disappears against my thighs. "I'll never forget how perfect your ass looks spread and on display for me."

His words alone send shivers across my body. "Zander..." I beg, hoping he'll move things along. "Need you."

Keeping a steady rhythm in and out of my soaked pussy, I hear what I've been waiting for. His wallet open and drop to the floor before the tines of his zipper sliding down.

"I have to stop touching you to put this on," he warns.

As much as I hate the loss of him, I'm eager for more.

From over my shoulder, I watch him rip the condom open and roll it over his long thick cock. "Ohmigod, this feels incredible," I mumble.

"It'll be even better when I can face you on a bed."

"Promises, promises," I tease. This is by far the sexiest thing I've ever done, and he hasn't even entered me yet.

"Tell me more about this fantasy of yours," he demands, leaning in to kiss my neck once more. Without warning, his fingers are back, playing with the walls of my pussy.

"Hmmm... it starts out like this," I say, rubbing my ass against his body. I feel his warm length against my ass and somehow, I'm even more turned on.

"And then," he prompts.

"Then you bring me to the brink with your hand, only to edge off. Then you'll do it again with your cock inside of me."

"It's like you've stepped out of my wet dreams into reality," he whispers. "Could you be any more perfect?"

Zander does exactly as I described—but brings it to an entirely new level.

The moment his thick cock enters me, I feel as if I might explode. Every nerve ending is a live wire as he waits for me to adjust to him. The heat from his body along my back as he leans against me to kiss my neck is beyond sensual. The moment his fingers find my clit, he circles the edge as he slides entirely around me.

Zander's deep voice takes things to an entirely new level when he demands, "Tell me what you need, Ari."

"You... just you," I beg.

I am not prepared for how full I feel with him. From this angle, my heels bring my ass to the perfect height for him—or so he says time and again as he works his way deep inside me. His fullness stretches me in just the right places and before I know it, I'm dying to move.

When he thinks I'm ready, he finally slides out slowly, then pivots and enters me again and again. Ohmigod, it's glorious. I meet him thrust for thrust and feel my orgasm build.

"God, Ari.... You feel incredible. Next time... I want to look in those beautiful eyes of yours and finally see all of you."

When he shifts his angle, he hits something deep inside me that I've never known existed.

I see stars. If I die in this moment, it will be the most miraculous way to go.

"Do that again," I mutter as I skyrocket over the edge into oblivion. Spasm after spasm rocks through me and it's all I can do to stay upright. After a few more thrusts, Zander stiffens and follows with me.

For a long moment, he holds me tight as our breathing returns to normal.

Turning to face him, he kisses me once more before sliding from my body.

"Be right back, don't move."

"Don't think I could if I tried," I mumble as I test the strength of my legs, which are about as strong as Jell-O at the moment.

Before he leaves, he whispers, "Let's get you out of these shoes, then get you cleaned up."

He quickly helps me slip off each shoe, then darts to the bathroom to dispose of the condom and brings back a washcloth. His pants are back on and I'm looking forward to taking my time to undress him—later. I can barely move at the moment though and if it wasn't for this door holding me up, I'd be a pile of goo on the floor.

Instead of handing me the clean cloth, he slowly bends and wipes up each of my legs and across my sex, then turns me to face him. And repeats the process with a dry towel, before letting me drop the skirt of my dress. He brushes a quick kiss across my lips.

"Next time we go from behind, I want a mirror in front of us so I can see your beautiful face."

Next time? He's already planning next time?

I can't even with this man.

"First, let's figure out how to unstick you from this dress."

Without a worry in the world, Zander carefully unpeels each part of my dress where I'd used double-sided tape. Then he helps me un-cinch the back of my dress and slowly step out of it.

Somehow, this entire process of him undressing me feels more intimate than actually having sex. But for some reason, I'm not at all uncomfortable with him seeing every part of me. Turning to face him, I look him over with care, then clear my throat to make my voice heard. "Uh.... You have entirely too many clothes on for our slumber party, Mr. Williams."

"We can't have that now," he says, kicking off his shoes and unbuttoning his fly, letting his pants drop to the floor.

The moment he takes my hand in his and leads me to the bed, the first of many more rounds begin, leaving me to finally drift off to sleep late into the night.

WHEN MY ALARM GOES OFF, I'd naturally roll over and hit snooze, but my body protests like I've worked out too hard and suddenly found muscles I'd forgotten existed. I vaguely remember Zander leaving earlier this morning but I was in a sex induced coma, filled with bliss, and didn't fully comprehend anything he said.

Fumbling with the hotel clock, I manage to move just enough to press snooze.

As a competitive athlete, the man has stamina and you'll

never hear me complain. I freaking lost track of how many orgasms we shared before I finally conked out on him.

I hope he at least got some sleep before leaving this morning.

Glancing at the dress that's slung against the back of the desk chair, I can't help but smile at remembering how hot our first time was. Here I'd thought Dylan and I had been somewhat adventurous in the bedroom, but I've never experienced anything like Zander. No, he took things to an entirely new level.

He could be Alpha-male one minute, making my core quiver in anticipation and completely sensual the next. After taking what we both desperately needed against the door, he was patient as we took off my dress. Then he ramped things up and after completely devouring my pussy with his mouth like he'd promised, he helped me pluck bobby pins from my hair for nearly twenty minutes before we explored the shower together.

The man is insatiable—and I loved it.

Just thinking about his gruff voice and his wicked tongue between my legs or hell—across my entire body has me aching with need and I seriously have no idea how it's even possible. I was well sated last night but somehow just the mere thought of being with him has my body responding to all things Zander.

Lying snuggled in the sheets that still smell like him, I inhale deeply. I seriously wish I could bottle this scent and return to this moment any time I needed a Zander fix.

Will I be needing a Zander fix though?

We never talked about where this left us. No—we were too

busy burning up the sheets, the shower, and every imaginable surface to actually talk about our feelings or where things would go from here.

I have zero regrets.

But the thought of not being with Zander leaves a dull ache in my chest.

I swear we were totally in sync this weekend. The way we connected and his ability to read my body like it was made just for him, would be a travesty to walk away from.

But what if this was just a one-time thing for him?

What if Zander started out as acting a part and things got carried away?

What if he's not looking for a relationship?

Do I even want a relationship?

Hell, am I even ready for one?

I mean, I brought a fake date to deal with Dylan for crying out loud.

Who does that?

But this fake dating was Zander's idea... he was already looking out for me. He cared about me enough—even as a friend to not let me go through this ordeal alone.

That has to mean something, right?

Maybe I wasn't ready for anything before this weekend started... but after everything I've learned about him this weekend... with Zander... I'm certain I could be.

I guess it all boils down to one question—Does he feel the same?

ZANDER

FROM THE MOMENT I stepped foot on campus Sunday morning, I've been on the go. My trainer kicked my ass because I was dog-tired when I arrived. I don't fucking regret a moment of my time with Ari, but he got the better of me in an instant. He knew something was off, but I wasn't about to tell him I'd been going on less than two hours of sleep, or he would've kicked my ass more than he already did.

To make matters worse, Ari didn't get back to campus until late Sunday evening and I was due on a bus first thing Monday morning for the airport. We've got two back-to-back games in Southern California, and we won't return home until late Wednesday evening.

I texted Ari when we landed in Cali Monday afternoon, but she was in class. Then she had tutoring sessions into the evening. We haven't actually talked at all the past two days, apart from a few—this isn't a good time texts. When she was free, I was in practice or sharing a room with DeShawn. The lack of privacy has never bothered me before, but with the way I left things between Ari and myself, I feel unsettled.

Thankfully, I've pulled it together on the court—so no one's the wiser of my misery. I'd give almost anything to talk to her. But fate's being a fickle bitch and it just hasn't worked out. God, what I'd give to see her beautiful face.

She might get a restraining order if she knew just how often I've stalked her social media or looked at the picture of us I swiped from the wedding. I don't wanna be a total creeper or completely presumptuous, so I haven't friended her on social media and simply kept to her public photos.

Honestly the phone won't work. This conversation must be done in person.

Though at this point, I'd settle to simply hear her voice. It's excruciating to be this far away and leave things between us unknown. It's crazy to think that in the span of a week, she's gone from being someone I have a working relationship with to someone I can't be without.

The kicker of it all, she doesn't have a clue how I feel about her.

No—I'm the dumbass who didn't take the time to tell her. I was too busy enjoying every sensation with her to actually make it known my feelings for her go far beyond physical. Don't get me wrong, sex with Ari is out of this world, but that's not all that I want from her. No. I want the entire package— brains, beauty, and friendship.

For all I know, she could be thinking I'm ghosting her, though I certainly hope that's not the case.

When I can't take it any longer, I pull up her contact info and tap out a text.

Me: Busy tomorrow night?

Shit, that sounds like a booty call.

Quickly I delete everything and try again.

Me: My flight gets in at six tomorrow. Can I stop by to talk?

Fuck. Talking sounds like I'm ending things.

Delete.

Me: Thinking of you.

Christ almighty, what the fuck do I say without looking like a complete idiot?

Delete.

Me: My flight gets in tomorrow at six. Can I see you when I get on campus?

Before I can overthink it, I hit send and power off my phone before stuffing it into my gear bag. I've got a game to win and need my attention focused on beating the Trojans—holy fuck. Even that's an innuendo.

I really hope I get things sorted with Ari sooner than later because I'm not sure how much longer I can handle this.

EVEN WITH OUR BACK-TO-BACK WINS, I'm still on pins and needles walking to my apartment. Thankfully, Ari's agreed to meet me, so I should be put out of my misery sooner than later. Since she has a roommate, I've invited her to my place. I'd rather have our much-needed conversation in private.

I hope like hell we're on the same page, but if we're not—I'd rather the world not see my disappointment.

She's been distant in her messages, though I guess I really haven't given her much to go by either—so I'm partially to blame. It's not like I really have anything to judge it by—as we never texted about anything but tutoring before our weekend at Seaside.

When I reach the bottom of my steps, movement by my door catches my attention and I'm frozen in place.

She's here—thirty minutes early.

My breath catches in my chest as I take her in.

There she is, in an oversized CRU sweatshirt and a pair of black skinny jeans. Her hair's piled on top of her head in a messy bun, and I swear she's never looked more beautiful than she is in this moment.

She's sitting on the top step with her elbows resting on her knees, looking at her phone. She's a sight for sore eyes and it's all I can do to not rush up the stairs, throw her over my shoulder, and carry her to bed. I need her desperately. But more importantly, I need to know we're okay.

I'm not sure how long I stare, wondering if I'm imagining this miracle, but when a car door closes behind me, she looks up and smiles. "There you are."

And I finally exhale.

"I wasn't expecting you so early," I admit, taking the steps two at a time.

Shrugging she stands. "I couldn't wait."

Stopping so that we're eye level, yet still a step apart, I ask hesitantly, "And why is that?" Somehow, I sound more nonchalant than I feel. My nerves are a jumbled mess and it's all I can do to stand in place. Grabbing the railing, I steady myself.

Scrunching her nose in the most adorable way she shrugs again. "I needed to see you."

"Need or want?" I ask, doing all I can to keep my hand on the rail.

Looking at the large bag slung over my shoulder, she suggests, "Why don't we go inside and talk."

Uh-oh. Nothing good ever comes of that.

Taking a step toward my door, I quickly unlock it.

"Before you *talk*, I have a few things I need to say."

Pushing the door open, I gesture for her to enter first, then point out, "My living room's off to the right." Dropping my bag on the floor, I close the door behind me and take a moment to gather the courage I'll need for this conversation.

My living room is the size of a postage stamp. I have a recliner and a couch I can stretch out on with a table between them. Both are centered with the TV as their focal point. It's not much of a place, but I'm proud to call it mine.

She steps toward me and I place a hand up to stop her—leaving her frozen in her tracks.

"Before you say anything, I need to get a few things off my chest."

Visibly, her posture straightens and for a split second, I almost chicken out.

"You see, Ari. You're an amazing tutor."

"Okay..." she draws out as her lower lip rolls under her teeth.

Shit. I'm fucking this up.

"Well... you started out as that... but then you turned into a friend..."

"I see..."

Fuck. I'm doing it again. Just come out and say it already, Zander. Stop beating around the bush. "Fuck it," I mutter more to myself than her.

Closing the distance between us, I reach for her hand. "Look. I'm royally fucking this up. The point I'm unsuccessfully attempting to make is that I like you.... As in... I really like you. As crazy as this sounds, I think I've pretty much fallen in love with you. You're all I think about. You consume nearly every part of my day that I'm not on the court. Hell, you're even featured in my dreams.... I'm not sure where you're at with us going forward as a couple. But I really hope we're on the same page. You once asked me if I've ever been in love... and at the time, I told you I haven't taken the time to get close enough to someone... and I'm fairly certain because I hadn't met you.... I..."

She places a finger over my lips and my words are cut off. "Are you ever going to let me talk?"

Gulping, I close my eyes and wait for her rebuttal.

"Open your eyes, Zander."

When I do, I'm met with the most gorgeous smile.

"If you stop rambling, you'd be happy to find I like you, too. In fact, I think you're pretty incredible. And absolutely adorable when you ramble like an idiot. I haven't been able to stop thinking about you either, and..." She nods eagerly. "Yeah... I'd like to make a go at this with you."

If I wasn't so eager to kiss her, I'd probably let out a whoop.

Closing the distance between us, I cup the back of her neck and guide her lips to mine.

When we're a mere breath apart, I whisper with a wide grin. "Best fucking words I've ever heard," before devouring her mouth with mine.

Ari

Two Years Later...

I SQUEAL when I spot Chloe coming down the aisle to meet me courtside for the opening game of the season. "I'm so glad you made it," I say in greeting. "It's been forever since we've hung out."

"You know how the off season goes." She laughs.

"Do I ever. During the season, games are predictable, but when he's off, Zander likes to cram as much into his time off as possible."

"From my understanding, Drew and Abby, Grey and Maddie, Tre and Margo are all coming tonight. We wouldn't miss the first game of the season where Zander and DeShawn face off professionally."

Zander was drafted into the NBA shortly after winning his second NCAA championship game. He's been playing ever since for the Vegas Jacks. Of course, I moved with him and I'm finishing up my master's in psychology at a private university here in town. I plan to specialize in anxiety disorders with children. Eventually, Zander and I will have kids, but I'd like to get married and finish school first.

This is DeShawn's first professional game. He was drafted last year for the Seattle Sailors and he and Chloe live outside of Seattle. She and I became close friends when she and DeShawn officially made a go of things—again—but that's her story to tell. We're both psychology majors and have a lot in common. I've also been able to help her become accustomed to the life of a professional basketball player as DeShawn redshirted his freshman year, so he didn't get drafted until the end of last season.

When the rest of our crew shows up, each couple is wearing a different jersey to show their support for the guys. I gotta love how Zander's group of friends support one another through thick and thin, even from afar. Drew and Abby traveled from the East coast to support their friends.

When each of the Jacks and Sailors come onto the court for warm-ups, we go wild. The crowd around us think we're nuts, but they have no idea how hard these men have worked to get to this place. Of course, this earns us an eye roll from each of them before they go to work warming up with their respective teams.

Right before each team is about to go in to the locker room for one final pep talk before the game, the announcer says, "Ladies and gentlemen. Can I have your attention." The crowd quiets for a moment before he continues, "If we could have a special point of privilege for a moment, there's something neither the players or the crowd will want to miss."

With that, both teams stop where they are and don't walk into the tunnel to their respective locker rooms.

"Ladies and gentlemen, will Ariadne Grable please come out to center court."

Suspiciously, I look to our friends and ask, "What the hell is going on?"

Everyone just shrugs as if they don't have a clue. Well, everyone but Chloe. She won't look me in the eye, so I'm certain she knows what's up.

"Ariadne Grable, would you please come to the center court for a special announcement," the announcer calls again and when I look out to the court, I spot myself looking scared shitless on the giant Jumbotron.

What the actual fuck is happening?

Knowing the entire arena's eyes are now on me, I stand on wobbly legs and walk out on to the court. The moment I step foot on the court, Zander walks through the tunnel holding a large bouquet of red roses.

How had I not noticed him leave?

It's not our anniversary. What the hell is he doing?

When he pulls out a cordless mic, I forget how to breathe. "Ari?"

Seeing that I'm frozen in place, he closes the distance and hands me the flowers.

"Ariadne Adel Grable—yes, this is important, so I'm full naming you.... You can get mad at me later." The arena erupts in laughter—so he waits for them to quiet down before continuing.

"From the moment I agreed to be your fake date at a wedding, I knew it would be more difficult than you'd ever imagine. You see—I already thought you were the most gorgeous woman in the room and had begun falling for you. I think I fell for your brain first, your handy highlighters second, and last but not least, your larger-than-life heart. You saw me for just me—and I knew... once you saw my dance moves, I'd have you hook, line, and sinker."

Again, the crowd laughs.

"I brought you out here tonight to ask you a very important question."

Before I can process, he drops to one knee.

"Ariadne Adel Grable, would you do me the honor of being my wife, my true partner in crime, and my life-long dance partner?"

With that, he digs into the pocket of his warm-up pants and pulls out a little black box. When he flips the lid, a stunning pear-shaped ring shines up at me. It's exactly what I would've picked out myself.

When I look into his eyes, my body unlocks from the statue I'd become and springs to his level. Throwing my arms around him, I whisper so that only he can hear, "Yes. Yes. Yes." Pulling back, I plant a kiss on his lips. "Yes, I'll marry you, Zander Williams."

THE END

Thank you for taking a chance on me as an author. I'd love to know what you think of Zander and to stay in touch. Please consider joining my Newsletter to make this possible. https://geni.us/AmandaShelleyNL

If you want more from this series, be sure to check out Drew: Book One of the Perfectly Independent Series where Drew's story continues...

Of all people, why him?

He didn't EVEN bother introducing himself, just assumed I knew him from his fame on the court.

Between his arrogance and the constant interruption from basketball groupies, there's no way I'll survive this semester. Sure, he's hotter than anyone I've ever laid eyes on in a science lab, but I can't afford to pull someone along to maintain the grade I deserve.

Just when I think my self-control is in check, he does something to remind me that he isn't the egotistical, self-centered jerk I thought he was.

With one stupid smile he makes my mind melt, my heart race, and my palms sweat.

Will my perfectly laid out plans disappear, if I take a chance on Drew?

Grab your copy today:

https://geni.us/AmandaShelleyBooks

Chapter One - Drew

DAMMIT, I'm late.

I hate being late.

Glancing at my watch, I know class hasn't started yet, and I still have some time, but it's been ingrained into me since I can remember—always show up early. Being on time is late—and today of all days, I need to be early.

I inwardly growl and readjust my backpack to pick up my pace.

From the moment I've walked into this building, I've been bombarded with fans. Sure, this is a D-1 school. I'm the captain of the basketball team and the lead scorer, so it's to be expected. But enough is enough. Of course, I'm noticed. It's not like I can help it. Being nearly six foot five is something I'm using to my advantage. I need to keep this scholarship and graduate with honors to get into med school. I know playing ball will only get me so far, and my dreams are bigger than that.

I like basketball, and I happen to be great at it. But ever since my sister died of Hodgkin's when she was twelve, I've had my heart set on becoming a doctor. I want to treat kids like her, with hopes of different outcomes. With her illness, my parents were up to their ears in debt. I've had to use my height and athleticism to get me where I am today—And I'm not taking any chances.

I've heard to choose my seat wisely on the first day of class. I need to get there to scout out the room. Not wanting another person to stop and discuss my last game, I keep my eyes trained on the floor, until I make it to the door.

Once inside, I'm relieved there are plenty of vacant seats still available. As I stop to look it over, I immediately notice a guy's face light with recognition, and I quickly dart my eyes away.

Nope. Not a chance.

Unfortunately, I've learned the hard way some fans can't get past my stats when I'm off the court. I need a partner who's focused. So, without a second's hesitation, I continue to survey the room for the person least likely to be a distraction.

Then I spot her.

From behind, she's non-descript. Her brown hair is tied into a ponytail, and she wears a plain white t-shirt, jeans, and Chuck Taylors. She isn't socializing with anyone, and with her large-framed glasses, she fits the bill for being the stereotype of studious.

As I approach, I find her focus unyielding. With her eyes locked onto the textbook in front of her, I can't help but smile. I need someone like her. When I pull out my stool and sit beside her, she doesn't even glance my way. It isn't until I greet her with, "Hey," she looks in my direction for the first time.

I smile and nod in greeting.

No recognition.

But her eyes lock with mine, and we stare at one another for a long moment.

Great. Maybe she does recognize me.

Should I look for somewhere else to sit? I glance around and find the tables around us are filling up.

But she grabs my attention when she finally mumbles, "Hey, I'm Abby."

I nod and grin in her direction. She clearly already knows my name.

A flicker of annoyance crosses her features before her expression turns blank, and she quickly returns her focus on her book. The corner of my lips pull up without my consent, but the moment I recognize it, I quickly school my features. She's just what I need her to be.

While we sit here, a guy I don't recognize stops by our table and high-fives me as he gushes, "Great game, man. You had me on the edge of my seat."

Not wanting to be rude, I shrug and accept the compliment. "Thanks. We were on fire last night. That's for sure." Then I make an exaggerated effort to pull out my notebook from my backpack.

I exhale heavily as he takes the hint and says, "You sure were. I'll see ya around." He looks in the direction of a vacant seat a few tables down, then returns a smile back at me. "Good luck next week."

"Thanks, man."

Abby continues reading her book in silence. But when a

string of people stop and congratulate me on our latest win, I notice when she balls her hands into fists a few times. I try to keep my conversations short, but as soon as a person leaves, I'm greeted by another. It's not like I can help it. I'm not about to be rude to fans, and it's not like class has started yet.

When another person approaches, I hear a loud huff from my side. But I do my best to ignore it. *She's obviously annoyed and just as focused as I need her to be.* I grin in amusement. My gut has never steered me wrong.

As this new guy greets me, the professor walks into the room, and relief washes through me. At least with class in session, people will leave me alone, and I can focus on why I'm here.

The professor stands in the center of the room for just a moment before clearing his throat. Everyone scatters to their seats as the aging man in the tweed jacket gathers some papers to put onto a podium. Once everyone's settled, the professor stands in front of the room and announces, "Good afternoon, ladies and gentlemen. Look to the person next to you. This is your permanent lab partner. There's no switching unless you want a ten percent reduction of your grade."

Gasps are heard around the room, and a light chuckle escapes from me as I glance to the girl next to me. Her jaw practically lands on the table, and it's all I can do to contain my amusement.

I manage to mumble, "It's a good thing I chose you for a partner then, isn't it?" as the professor launches into discussing the syllabus as well as his expectations for the semester.

Somehow, Abby manages to regain her composure, and the two of us spend the remainder of class taking copious notes. Abby's diligent, and that's just what I need with the season getting started and my full course load to stay on track for graduation.

Typically, athletes take fewer credits during the season, but if I'm to graduate on time and get into the school of my dreams, I can't afford to slow my pace. As it is, I'm already busting my butt and have had to take summer classes to get the extra classes necessary for admissions.

When class ends, Abby quickly gathers her things and abruptly stands. She won't even look in my direction as she makes her way out of the room. I can't help but stare after her and wonder what our next class will bring.

Chapter Two - Abby

When I return to lab the following Tuesday, I'm quickly reminded of how I left. To avoid any conversation with my extremely popular lab partner, I stormed out of the classroom, wondering how I'll get through this semester.

He might not be that bad, but the string of people who kept stopping by... No, thank you.

Unfortunately, I remember the professor's words all too

well. I can't afford a drop in my grade, especially this early in the semester.

It's only one semester, Abby. You can do this.

Of all the places he could sit, why did he choose my table? When he mumbled something about specifically choosing me, what the hell did he mean by that?

Shit, is he planning on using me like Toby did my sophomore year?

Christ. I can't go through that again. There's no way in hell, I'd survive. I'm already taking twenty credits and working as many hours as I can at the library. I can't afford to pull someone along to maintain the grade I deserve. Don't even get me started on how it felt to be used emotionally either.

Been there, done that. Don't need the t-shirt.

When I walk in, I'm relieved to find my table empty. I sit and unpack my things to settle in for class. I'm reviewing this week's reading assignment to make sure it's fresh in my mind when the hair on the back of my neck pricks. As if my body knows he's here before I consciously do, I'm alerted to the scrape of a stool next to me.

I smile a greeting in his direction.

Maybe today will be different?

He nods once, then digs into his backpack, and for the most part, ignores me.

The smell of his cologne permeates the air, and my stomach does a small involuntary flip. I take a moment to take him in, realizing I might not have given him a fair chance the last time we met.

Okay, I'll admit it, the man's hotter than anyone I've ever

laid eyes on in a science lab. His dark hair makes his blue eyes pop and smolder. His large frame fills out the black shirt he's wearing, as if it's been tailor made for his well-defined chest underneath. His square jaw with just the right amount of scruff and perfect lips are set in a straight line. When my gaze finally returns to his eyes, I find him staring expectantly. *Holy hell! Get it together, Abby. He's just a guy. But why did he choose to sit by me?*

To regain control over my body's reaction to the mysterious man sitting next to me, I quickly return my attention to my book. Though let's be honest, I've hardly read more than a page since he made his presence known.

My ability to focus is thwarted by his sexy masculine scent and the unpacking of his materials for class. From the corner of my eye, I can't help but watch his every move. As he pulls out a notebook, his muscular arms flex, and his elbow slightly brushes my arm, sending shivers down my spine.

Just like last time, people continue to stop and chat with him before class begins. My mind drifts to our last encounter, and I grimace.

I'm quickly reminded of how he thought he was too important to be bothered to mention his name... *and how my instant crush ended.* The man may be hot as hell, but he's one of the cockiest people I've ever met, and that's a major turnoff. Hell, I don't have time to date, even if he wasn't so arrogant, so it's a moot point.

As our professor gets lab started, I'm relieved to find the guy next to me may be a jock, but at least he isn't a dumb jock. He's able to hold his own when it comes to our chemistry lab. We work solidly together until the professor announces we can take a short break and leave when we're through.

"Do you mind if we work through the break? I have someplace I have to be after class," Mr. No Name asks.

I'd ask his name but after working with him for the past hour, it's just beyond weird to ask now. Maybe he'll get called something other than Dude, or Man and I can figure it out, when the time comes.

Knowing I have work later, I eagerly agree but keep our extraneous conversation to a minimum. "Sounds great."

We work diligently until a steady stream of people flock over to converse again about the latest game. Mr. Socialite is all smiles as he greets them. I try not to let it bother me, but after the fourth interruption, I finally lose it and feel the need to remind him of the commitment he's made.

In an attempt to regain control of my emotions and not sound like a complete bitch, I take a deep breath, but it comes out as a huff instead. This immediately gets the attention of Mr. Blue Eyes, who's now staring in my direction. I almost lose my nerve when I see the smile form on his perfectly shaped lips. *Who the hell is this guy?*

"Okay, *partner*," I spit out. "Are we doing this, or what?" I look pointedly at the lab in front of us. "You said we needed to get done early because you had places to be. You're too busy being Mr. Socialite to get anything done."

Instead of his smile fading, it grows into a smirk. "I knew you'd keep me on track." I glance around, and everyone has dispersed. "I just might keep you around."

"Keep me around?" There's no way I heard him correctly. "What do you mean by that?"

"I made the right choice by sitting here. You won't let distractions stop us, and you can pull your weight on the labs." He shrugs his shoulders, as if that should explain everything.

How should I respond to that?

Thankfully, my irritated vibe must project throughout the room because we're no longer bothered by any unwelcome guests. A sense of satisfaction spreads over me as we finally delve back into our project.

When our work is finished, we make use of the remaining time going over required assignments. Blue Eyes (yes, that's what I'm calling him since I still don't know his name) and I decide we'll need to meet outside of class to get a few things done.

When I suggest meeting at the library or local coffee shop, he hesitates and looks around.

"What?" I ask, not understanding his reaction.

"Well..." His chagrin look surprises me. He glances around the room once again. *What is it that makes him think everyone is watching?* "Can you think of anywhere less... public?"

How big of him to not want to be seen with the likes of me. *What a cocky-ass!* "If you'd rather do this on your own, go ahead. We'll just split up the work." After spending time working with him today, I'm confident he'd do the quality of work I expect from myself.

"Um..." His expression is unreadable for a split second before he continues, "I want to complete it together."

"So, you want to collaborate but not be seen with me in

public? Exactly how am I supposed to take that?" My defenses are up. If this douche canoe wants my help but doesn't want to be seen with me, he's got another thing coming.

"Ohmigod, no," he quickly replies. He suddenly looks apologetic, which catches me off guard. "This has nothing to do with being seen with you. It's just... me..."

"Oh, so the 'it's not you, it's me' speech." I shake my head in disgust. I thought we'd gotten along fine for our lab, but this takes the cake. "Wow. That's rich." I pack up my things. I'm not putting up with his crap. I have better things to do this afternoon.

I stand to leave, but he captures my wrist as I do. There's a spark of electricity pulsing between us, holding me in place.

"Abby, let me explain," he pleads. His blue eyes pierce through me as if he's searching for the words, as I remain frozen in place.

"Go for it, Blue Eyes," I say without any thought.

"It's Drew." His lashes lower as he looks somewhat humble —sort of. The jury's still out until I hear what he has to say. I shake my head at his statement, wondering what the hell he's talking about.

"My name. It's Drew. There's no problem being seen with you. Before you jumped to conclusions, I'm trying to explain how public places tend to get hectic. You've only seen a glimpse of what it's like." He looks around the room as if that's an explanation. "I think it would be best to meet somewhere out of the public eye, for your sake... So we won't have as many distractions."

"Oh." What can I say to that?

"Come to my place. We can avoid groupies," he suggests with a shrug.

"You want me... to come to your place?" I stare at him, surprised. Then another thought hits me. "You have... groupies?"

Drew looks as if he's unsure of himself. As I look into his eyes, trying to read his expression, I suddenly realize how tall he is. My neck hurts to look up at him. How tall is he? I'm five-ten, and I'm a dwarf to him in comparison.

He shakes his head, breaking my internal inquiry about the giant before me. "Christ, this is more difficult than it has to be." He looks around before whispering, "I promise nothing will happen to you at my house. I'm on a tight schedule with practice, and I don't have time to traipse all over campus trying to find a private place to work."

"Well, this is unexpected," I mumble. A thousand questions come to mind, but not knowing where to start, I just stare.

He takes my silence as needing further explanation. He spends the next few minutes quickly explaining how his popularity has risen since their championship game last season. He tells me it's hard for him to blend in as a typical guy on campus. I have no doubts of that because come on... look at him. He may be arrogant as hell, but he's ultimately a beautiful giant. Though I'd never admit that part to him aloud.

Drew's voice is low and deep when I finally concede to his request. "You mentioned having to work tonight. What about tomorrow night? We need to get the first assignment done before I leave Friday morning with the team. It's due on Monday, and I won't be back until Sunday afternoon."

Shit! Of course, he chooses tomorrow night. It's my only night off this week, and I already have plans. Though… my plans won't happen until later. Maybe I can squeeze in a study session to finish this assignment. Knowing it's our only option, I sigh in defeat. "Okay. Tomorrow will work. Can we make it early because I have plans later?"

Drew's blue eyes widen for a fraction of a second, but it's quickly replaced with relief. "Sure. Give me your phone number, and I'll text my address. Practice ends at six, would seven work for you?"

I'll have to figure out dinner on my own. Not sure my friends will understand, but they'll get over it—hopefully. We weren't planning to leave until eight, so it should be fine. I nod in agreement and give him my number. Within seconds, a notification arrives on my phone. Knowing it's likely him, I keep it in my pocket.

"Thanks." Drew sighs with relief as he gathers his things. "I gotta get to practice. But I'll see you then."

I let out a heavy sigh, knowing my friends might kill me for changing our dinner plans. "Sounds good. I'll have to leave as soon as we finish. My friends will be expecting me."

"Hey, Abby?" Drew asks hesitantly. "Would you mind keeping my number between us? I'd rather not share it with everyone."

"There go my plans for writing it on the bathroom stall," I mumble sarcastically. Drew just stares. His dark eyebrows pinched. Apparently, my humor's lost on him. I quickly put him at ease. "Just kidding," I assure him, and his perfect lips quirk into a smile. With that, he leaves our table, leaving me to stare after him.

WHEN I GET to my apartment after work that evening, I throw my backpack onto the couch and plop down beside it. My roommate Chloe looks up from the kitchen table where she's studying and asks, "That bad?"

"Yes," I say in a groan. "I have the worst lab partner this term."

"Tell me more," she prompts. Chloe's a psychology major and has been one of my best friends since summer camp in seventh grade. She likes to use what she's learning in class on me, so I stick my tongue out at her to let her know I can see she's up to her usual antics. She bursts out with laughter. *Great. Just what I need.* "Seriously, Abs, tell me what's going on. There must be more to this than a crappy lab partner. This is so unlike you."

"Uggh," I groan in frustration. It would've been so simple if only he'd chosen a different seat.

When I don't say anything, Chloe merely lifts a perfectly sculpted eyebrow and waits.

"Well..." I start, not knowing where to begin. Taking a deep breath, I let it all out, knowing I might as well start from the beginning. "It all started on the first day of class. This *guy...*" I say with disdain, causing Chloe to smirk, but I ignore her. "Plopped down next to me and didn't say anything but 'hey.' Then as if he's Mr. Popularity himself, he has a constant string of people stopping by to talk about his latest game. It was soooo frustrating. They wouldn't go away. As soon as one person left, it was like it signaled another to drop by. *Just when I think it couldn't get any worse*, the professor walks in and makes an announcement that was like a bomb detonating. The person next to us has just become a permanent partner for the term, unless we want a ten percent reduction in grade... You know I can't have that. I need straight As or med school's no longer an option." I inhale sharply and take a breath. But I can't help but cringe when I think of what I must tell her next.

"But that's not even the worst part. We must finish up a project before Friday, and the only night the almighty Drew is available, is tomorrow night. Can you believe that?"

"Um..." Chloe puts her index finger on her chin and pretends to think something over. "What part of this is supposed to be bad enough to put you into such a pissy mood?"

My eyes nearly pop out of my head as it snaps in her direction. "That's how you're going to handle clients one day?" I ask in disbelief. Chloe's known for her zero BS policy, but this is a bit over the top, even for her.

"You're going to miss me next year, and you know it. It's all your fault, you're a Brainiac and will graduate earlier than the rest of us."

Yeah, I came into CRU with enough credits to graduate a year early, but she's known that since—forever—so I simply roll my eyes and wait for a real response.

"Well, since you know me *too* well, you'll never be my client, but... I think there's more than what you've just told me at play here. What's really going on?" Her brown eyes widen as she waits expectantly.

I shake my head and stare at my feet, now propped up on the coffee table. "I... Uh... have to cancel our dinner plans tomorrow night. I must study with *him,* at seven. It shouldn't take long to finish our project, but I won't be able to meet you until afterward."

"Girl, you're *not* bailing on us tomorrow night." Chloe steps up from the table, and her oversized scoop-neck top slips off one shoulder. She comes to stand in front of me at the couch as she eyes me suspiciously. "We all coordinated our schedules to celebrate *you.* This is a once in a lifetime thing. You can't ditch us. Syd will be pissed."

I shake my head, knowing she's right but trying to make her see she's not hearing me correctly. "I'll be there. There's no doubt about that. I'll just have to meet you after dinner. That's all. I looked over the assignment, and it really shouldn't take Drew and me too long to complete."

As if she doesn't believe me, Chloe cocks her head to the side and eyes me suspiciously. "Are you sure you're not trying to ditch us? I know you didn't want to go out. But this is a big deal. You *have* to go with us."

Internally I groan, though I keep that thought to myself. "Chloe, I won't miss this. I promise."

"If you do, Sydney will kick your ass." Chloe tries to keep a serious face but completely fails, causing both of us to break into laughter.

Sydney's our other roommate. She's been one of my closest friends since freshman year. She lived across the hall from us in the dorms. She's taking tomorrow night off, which is rare for her. I know she needs the money. I also know they want to celebrate together. This only comes along once in a lifetime.

"I know it's important. I'll be there," I promise.

Chapter Three - Drew

Abby's stubborn. But she's also tenacious. She remembers facts and numbers like nobody I've ever met. It's almost as if she has a photographic memory. I can only wish my mind worked as well as hers. For the most part, Abby sticks to business, and I get little in terms of reading her personality beyond having an amazing work ethic.

As I contemplate our conversation in class, I can't help but smile. It took me a while to explain that I play basketball, and since we won the championship game last season, my popularity's skyrocketed. I can't be a random guy on campus anymore. Her feisty attitude and unwillingness to take my shit is quite intriguing. I couldn't help but laugh when she asked, "How do you expect to blend in as a giant?"

I've been a starter here at Columbia River University since freshman year. I didn't redshirt because I don't intend to play in the NBA. I'm here to get my degree. However, the fame that comes with winning is a double-edged sword. It opens doors for me, but being unable to be a regular guy on campus is unnerving.

I don't usually date during the season to avoid distractions. The number of trolls who venture into the arena to simply chase jerseys is unbelievable. I distance myself from the social side of being a college athlete by keeping my head in the game and focusing on my studies. Besides, this keeps the girls away who aren't interested in getting to know the *real* Drew Jacobs.

When there's a knock at my door, promptly at seven, I rush to greet Abby. I'm blown away by how different she looks. Standing before me is a beautiful girl with long, wavy, brown hair and brown eyes I can see. She's wearing a fitted blue sweater that accentuates her curves and a faded pair of denim jeans that are worn in just the right places. The only resemblance to my nerdy lab partner is her Chuck Taylors.

"Abby?" I state, but it comes out like a question. *So much for not being a distraction. I'm so fucking screwed.* Of course, my cock chooses this moment to spring to attention. I've never been more thankful for wearing jeans, as my basketball shorts leave little to the imagination.

"Drew?" She stares for a moment. "Planning on letting me in?"

WANT to know what happens next to Drew and Abby? You can start reading their complete story today in Drew: Book One of the Perfectly Independent Series.

https://geni.us/ASDrew

ABOUT THE AUTHOR

Amanda Shelley loves falling into a book to experience new worlds. As an avid reader and writer, sharing worlds of her own creation is a passion that has inspired her to become an author. She writes contemporary romance with characters who are strong and sexy with a touch of sass.

When not writing, Amanda enjoys time with her family, playing chauffeur, chef, and being an enthusiastic fan for her children. Keeping up with them keeps her alert and grounded. She enjoys long car rides, chai lattes, and popping her SUV into four-wheel drive for adventures anywhere.

Amanda loves hearing from readers. Be sure sign up for her newsletter and follow her on social media. Join her reader's group *Amanda's Army of Readers* to stay up to date on her latest information.

Readers group: https://www.facebook.com/groups/Amandas
ArmyofReaders/
Goodreads: https://www.goodreads.com/author/show/
19713563.Amanda_Shelley
Newsletter: https://geni.us/AmandaShelleyNL
www.amandashelley.com

interruption from basketball groupies, there's no way I'll survive this semester.

Sure, he's hotter than anyone I've ever seen in a science lab with his sexy blue eyes, cute dimple, and muscles for days - but I can't afford *his* kind of distractions.

Okay. Deep breath.

I can do this.

After all, it's only one semester.

Just when I think my self-control is in check, he does something to show me that he isn't the egotistical, self-centered jerk I thought he was.

How can his stupid smile suddenly make my mind melt, heart race, and palms sweat?

If I take this chance on Drew, will my perfectly laid out plans disappear?

https://geni.us/AmandaShelleyBooks

Vince: Book Two of the Perfectly Independent Series

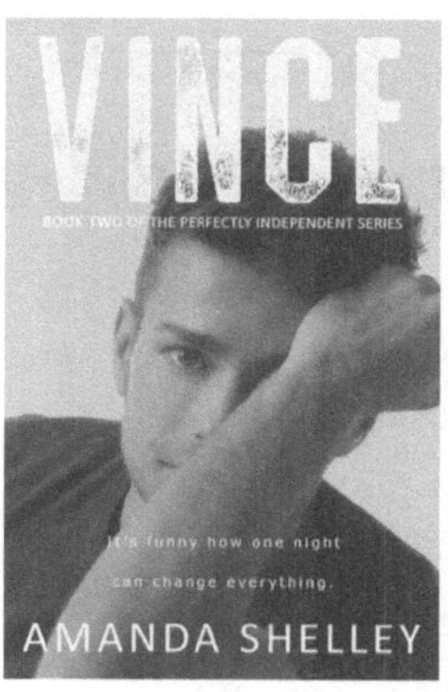

It's funny how one night can change everything.

As a bartender near campus, I'm certain I've heard it all. Rarely a shift passes without some guy taking his best shot, hoping I'll end my self-proclaimed dating diet.

Of course, this is exactly how I meet Vince.

Except, he isn't the one running his mouth.

No, he simply shuts down his idiotic friend, then stops my heart with the simplest of smiles and walks away.

Just when I force myself to forget him, he bumps into me on campus.

Our connection is consuming, and my world is knocked off kilter. It's far beyond physical attraction. He's smart, sexy, and feels like—home?

Wait, that can't be right...

Whatever it is, Vince has me breaking my rules to spend time with him.

My entire life I've prepared for meeting the wrong guys.

What the hell should I do when I find the right one?

https://geni.us/AmandaShelleyBooks

Damien: Book Three of the Perfectly Independent Series

Beautiful girls are not hard to find at Columbia River University.

The coeds on campus are great to look at but I was over that scene after graduation three years ago.

These days, outside of being part of the largest civil engineering job on campus, all I'm searching for is a decent meal and some peace and quiet. It's why I'm happy to have found what I consider a hidden gem in the diner I frequent.

All I need to do is finish this job and move on to the next by year's end.

Should be easy enough. Only when Vanessa walks up with a sexy smile and a mouth full of sass, she does more than take my order. She completely takes my breath away.

Next thing I know, I'm here every morning, making every excuse to dine with this intriguing woman. Not only is she smart and sexy, but she's laser focused on reaching the goals she's set for herself.

The more I get to know her, the more I'm convinced she's the one. I just have to find a way to get her to deviate from her perfectly laid plans and take a chance on me.

https://geni.us/AmandaShelleyBooks

Making The Call

Dani

As a bestselling romance author, most assume my life's glamorous, filled with combustible chemistry, and most of all, romance. Ha! I can only wish. With a deadline looming, I've escaped to my family's cabin on Anderson Island to free myself from distractions. My plan's great, until a man, who could pass as a cover model on one of my books, comes to my rescue. Is there chemistry? Sure. Is he everything I'd look for in a guy? Absolutely. But will my career be at risk if I give into my desire?

Luke

For a player, women line up outside the locker room. For coaches, we're lucky to get in the game. As the youngest NFL coach in the league, I live, eat, breathe, and even sleep football. To gear up for this season, I return to my home on Anderson Island for a much-needed break. When Dani literally crashes into my life, my mind's suddenly on the sexy brunette with a sailors mouth, rather than my team's next play. She has me dusting off another playbook entirely, making me wonder, did I make the right call?

https://geni.us/AmandaShelleyBooks

The Summer Dare

Leave it to Nana to think of everything.

After a grueling semester, I'm ready for a peaceful summer in Seaside with my sisters.

Imagine my surprise, when I'm woken by the screeching sound of a saw coming through my wall, the first official morning of break.

Not only did I come flying out of bed swinging, but I gave Ryan, the unsuspecting carpenter the surprise of his life, when I came wielding my killer coat hanger and all.

Too bad, I was only in a tank and undies and it wasn't nearly as effective as I'd hoped.

Of course, he insists he's only doing his job. Since it's Nana's last request to care for us, I can't refuse.

However, I won't let a tall, pesky, sexy as sin, know-it-all get in my way of my summer plans. I pretend I ignore him – that is until my youngest sister pokes her nose in my business and throws down a dare I can't back down from.

Kiss the next single guy who walks up to the bonfire – or explain to my sisters why I get riled up over the contractor.

When Ryan suddenly appears, I know I'm screwed in more ways than one.

Not only will my sisters learn my secret, but from the determined look on Ryan's face, I'm afraid he's eager to reveal it to the world as well.

What have I gotten myself into?

As I walk toward him, one thing is certain – this summer dare will either make or break me.

https://geni.us/AmandaShelleyBooks

My sisters are dropping like flies.

They're falling in love and having the time of their lives.

Don't get me wrong, I'm ecstatic for them. I love seeing them happy.

But I'm not ready for that type of commitment.

I can't even keep a plant alive, let alone find someone worthy of getting past a third date.

As the only sister done with school and single as a pringle, I have to do something fast, or I'll be my matchmaking aunt's next victim.

When Jax's drummer joins him for the summer and needs some help with his image, I make him a deal he can't refuse.

All is perfect—until I realize my summer proposal has one minor flaw.

Our relationship may be a sham, but there's nothing fake about my feelings for Finn.

https://geni.us/AmandaShelleyBooks

The Summer Arrangement

One, two, three—it's all down to me.

As the youngest and only single Lancaster, I'm eager to spend my summer in Seaside, Oregon, with my sisters. It's something I've looked forward to all year, and I'm determined to make every minute count. After all, I've only got one year before I graduate from college and have to adult for real.

However, if I want to graduate debt free, I need to work. I have a lead on the perfect summer job with the nanny agency I've spent the last three summers catering to.

I just have to win over an adorable three-year-old and convince her single dad I'm the right one for the job.

Simple enough, right?

Except when I show up at his door, I'm shocked to find he's the guy I hooked up with a few times last semester.

This cannot be happening.

I need this job. There's too much on the line to walk away. Maybe we can put the past behind us and make some sort of summer arrangement?

https://geni.us/AmandaShelleyBooks

The Summer I Found Home

Being a pilot is all I've ever known.

I served my country and I'm damn proud of my career.

But sacrifices were made, especially when it came to family.

I've missed first steps, first days of school, and first dates to name a few.

My kids grew up. They're having families of their own.

Was it worth it?

When an opportunity brings me to Seaside, I jump feet first no questions asked.

It means experiencing all those firsts with my grandkids.

With family as my focus and my guard down, I don't even see Faye coming.

She's a force to be reckoned with and has me holding on for dear life.

I thought our ship had sailed, but now that I'm home for good—I just might get more than one second chance.

arrangement?

https://geni.us/AmandaShelleyBooks

The Boy Upstairs

I ran into Derek while trying to escape the neighbor from hell.

Instantly, we hit it off. Since he's only here for three months and the microbrewery leaves me little time for commitments, it's the perfect setup for a fling.

He's adventurous, challenges me, and he just gets me from the inside out.

With our expiration date quickly approaching, I'm left to wonder...
Will my heart ever be the same without the boy upstairs?

https://geni.us/AmandaShelleyBooks

He Saved My Boy

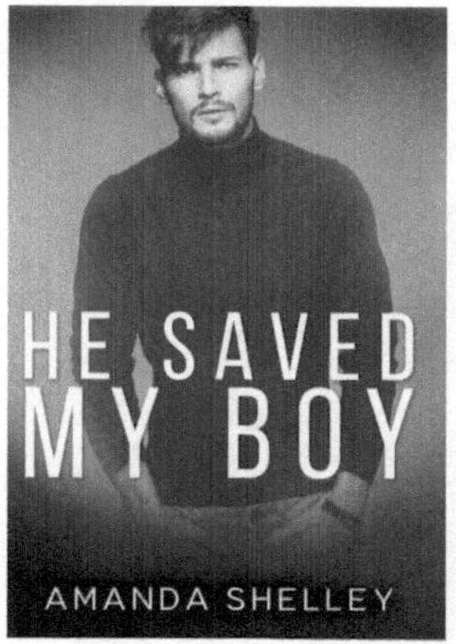

Davis is the first guy to catch my attention since... hell, I don't even
know.

Instantly, he makes me think and feel things I've forgotten existed. It
has been forever since I put my needs first, so I take the chance and let
him light me up from the inside out.

Our night is the kind that will ruin me for all others.

But then I get the dreaded call.

I rush out without a second glance, knowing I'll likely never see him
again.

My son will always come first—Always.

Imagine my surprise when Davis walks in, and I find he's the only one who can save my boy.

This cannot be happening—*I guess it's time to pull up my big girl panties and see what happens.*

https://geni.us/AmandaShelleyBooks

The Vegas Pitch

This pitch could make or break my career.

Not only will it set a personal record for the biggest account I've ever landed, but it could set my newfound company three years ahead of schedule for expansion.

Thank god I've got Nate Bellinger on my team.

Even though I had my reservations hiring the sexiest man I've ever laid eyes on – he more than meets my expectations with his hard work and determination. Together, we've formed a solid team and play off each other perfectly.

As we wait for the final verdict, I begrudgingly take Nate up on his offer for a night on the town. After all, this is Vegas and I need to let the chips fall where they may.

Imagine my surprise when I wake up the next morning to find we've not only won the campaign, but I'm apparently married to the man I've only ever let myself fantasize about.

The kicker of it all – he has no intentions of letting me go.

But what will it mean once we leave Vegas?

https://geni.us/AmandaShelleyBooks

Resilience: Book One of Resilience Duet

Resolution: Book Two of Resilience Duet

Samantha never saw Enzo coming.

As the dust settles from her divorce, her life is full. She doesn't have time for distractions. She's too busy running her own company and checking off numerous items from her kids' demanding schedule to have a life of her own.

Then he walks into her kitchen with his breathtaking green eyes and a mischievous grin. He's there to surprise his father - her contractor, but his presence makes everything off kilter.

Enzo's perfectly content with his adventurous life as an elite rescue pilot, until a harmless prank turns on him. Instead of surprising his father, he finds his world thrown off course by the beautiful woman with a sexy smile, wicked sass and the mouthwatering ability to keep him on his toes.

With his limited time on leave, is she worth the risk to his heart?

https://geni.us/AmandaShelleyBooks

Collide: A Sweet Romance

Falling head over heels was the last thing I expected.

Literally.

Coffee is everywhere – and more than my ego is bruised.

When the handsome stranger I plowed into calls me by name, mortification sinks in.

He rushes off to class. I run home to change, hoping to forget the whole incident.

If only I could be so lucky.

I quickly find it's a small world and Gavin Wallace is completely unavoidable. Everywhere I turn he's there. In my classes. Hanging with my friends.

I've got his full attention and I have to admit, I like it a lot more than I should.

https://geni.us/AmandaShelleyBooks